TREK
the lost years

Edited and Designed by Hal Schuster

Cover painting by Dameon R. Willich

TREK
the lost years

BY JAMES VAN HISE

PIONEER BOOKS   LAS VEGAS, NEVADA

All correspondence: 5715 North Balsam Road, Las Vegas, Nevada 89130.

TREK: THE LOST YEARS

FIRST PRINTING: JUNE 1989

10 9 8 7 6 5 4 3 2 1

Dedicated to Timmie, a new generation of Trekkers.

CONTENTS

THE LOST YEARS.

Sounds like an alcoholic or drug addict who has suddenly gone straight, and looks back at the wasted years left behind; years which prove irretrievable and serve as a powerful reminder of the depths to which the human soul can plunge. And while it lacks the gravity of these examples, the attempted revival of **Star Trek** of the mid-Seventies can be looked upon as lost years, where dreams were often smashed by egos, and creativity stifled by greed. Yet, by the same token, it was a time of magic, when the attempt was made to catch lightning in a bottle for a second time.

In all probability, the general public looks upon the success of both **Star Trek V: The Final Frontier** and the television series **Star Trek: The Next Generation** as something fairly commonplace; nothing out of the ordinary. Additionally, they probably look back at the first film (1979's **Star Trek: The Motion Picture**) and think that some whiz-kid at Paramount Pictures sat down, happened to watch an episode of the original series and heard the voice of God telling him that it would be a great idea to bring the cast back together in a feature film. "It would be fun," the whiz-kid would have reasoned, "and nostalgic, and bring people back to an earlier period of their lives.

"Oh yeah," he could be heard adding, perhaps a bit more softly, "we could also make a few bucks off of it."

And thus, the public believes, the **Star Trek** movies were born.

Unfortunately, this emphatically was *not* the case.

The revival of **Star Trek** was a grueling ten year period of endless promises and false starts, and it's a miracle creator Gene Roddenberry and the cast of actors did not suffer nervous breakdowns. Consider the fact that the original **Star Trek** television series had become so much a part of the popular culture that the actors, with the exception—to some degree—of William Shatner and Leonard Nimoy, were forever typecast. No matter what small parts might come along, this group would be forever known as the crew of the starship Enterprise. This left an ensemble of sev-

> " The revival of **Star Trek** was a grueling ten year period of endless promises and false starts. "

11

en fine actors who, via their indelible abilities, had managed to bring the characters to startling life, but now couldn't find work anywhere else.

The price, you might say, of fame. But what about the price of food? Housing? Education for their kids?

Fine. So you've got seven actors known for particular roles, and you have millions of fans just waiting for the opportunity to see them reprise those roles. Even if you were looking at it from only a financial standpoint, you're talking about millions of potential dollars. The course seems obvious, so what was the problem? Why did it take **Star Trek** so long to make a comeback?

That, my friends, will remain one of the great unanswered questions of all time.

As early as 1973, rumors circulated that the show would be returning in one form or another. Eventually Paramount and NBC produced a Saturday morning animated series, but that didn't really cut it. Sure it was great to hear the voices of the cast reprising their roles in semi-literate scripts, but what about a live action adventure dealing with the nature of the human soul or the universe itself?

In the ensuing years, there would be no less than five attempts to bring **Star Trek** back, before it was decided to produce the first feature film. Early in the seventies, Paramount was afraid that the show's popularity was merely a fad, and that it would vanish by the time a film made it to the screen. Then, when they realized that there was no end to the growing popularity of their property in sight, they couldn't decide what to do with it. Gene Roddenberry has joked that the studio wanted something like "Star Trek Versus Godzilla," and one executive reportedly asked Harlan Ellison to add Mayans to his story idea, despite the fact that the story had nothing whatsoever to do with Mayans. The executive merely felt that since *Chariots of the Gods* was so popular at the time, it might be a good idea to add Mayans so as to make a science fiction film taking place in the 23rd Century look contemporary.

Then **Star Wars** reached theaters in 1977, and rapidly became the number one grossing film in history. Paramount observed this, released a corporate sigh and said, "Guess we're too late."

Plans were made for a brand new syndicated television series entitled **Star Trek II**, which would reunite most of the original cast

> 66
>
> In the ensuing years, there would be no less than five attempts to bring **Star Trek** back.
>
> 99

and launch a brand new five year mission, but Steven Spielberg's **Close Encounters of the Third Kind** was released, and it, too, proved itself to be a high-grossing success. Once again, Paramount watched, scratched its corporate chin and changed its collective mind. One week before shooting on the new series was scheduled to commence, the studio decided that it would be better served financing a big budget feature film with a distinguished director at the helm.

In December of 1979, **Star Trek: The Motion Picture** finally made it to the screen after a ten-year struggle, leaving in its wake a variety of unused screenplays and teleplays. Since that time, of course, there have been an additional four films and two seasons of the aforementioned **Star Trek: The Next Generation**, all of which indicate that the phenomenon will live well into the 21st Century.

Star Trek: The Lost Years is an examination of the events between the cancellation of the original series in 1969 and the announcement of the movie a decade later. In these pages, you'll meet the behind-the-scenes personnel of the adventures you never saw, and learn of the Enterprise voyages that might have been. Purists may be outraged that our focus is not on the cast of actors from the series, but it's important to note that throughout this period, it was the *behind-the-scenes* drama that would ultimately decide the future of **Star Trek**.

The Lost Years are the final frontier of the **Star Trek** mythology; a ten year period which has never truly been explored. Certainly there has been occasional mention in various publications, but never before has its full wealth been examined in such detail. This is a special journey filled with numerous surprises; one guaranteed to take you where no fan has gone before.

I hope you enjoy this excursion into the **Star Trek** universe.

**Edward Gross,
January 1989**

From the outset, it should have been obvious to everyone that **Star Trek** would be unlike any other television series ever aired. After all, the show marked the first time that a network had rejected a pilot, while still funding a second one. In essence, NBC gave series creator Gene Roddenberry that all too rare opportunity of a second chance.

As fans of **Star Trek** are well aware, the series never really garnered strong ratings, struggling through its first two seasons. By the end of the second year, NBC announced that they were cancelling the show. A phenomenal letter writing campaign ensued which "forced" the network to reconsider its decision and renew the show for a third season. Such a ploy had been unprecedented at the time, although, more recently, both **Cagney and Lacy** and **Designing Women** have been saved through similar means.

In 1968, Gene Roddenberry, worried the network axe would prevent the Enterprise from completing her five year mission, made a promise to NBC: if they continued production of the series, he would come back and personally produce the show, guaranteeing them the quality would return to that of the first season. During that same year, he spoke to an audience at Berkley, explaining the situation.

"You all know we won the fight," he said, stressing that the show would be returning for a third season. "At that time I told them that if they would put us on the air as they were promising—on a weeknight at a decent time slot, 7:30 or 8:00—I would commit myself to produce **Star Trek** for the third year. Personally produce the show as I had done at the beginning. This was my effort to use what muscle I had. The networks were monolithic, multibillion dollar corporations whose interests are not necessarily in the quality of the drama. Basically, the hard facts of life in television, and this one you must understand, is that a show is bought or sold on how much toothpaste or underarm deodorant will that show sell. Basically that is why a show is bought and how it is kept on the air.

"If a creator, a writer, were to come along and come up with a big significant visual imagery," he continued, "the finest thing you could think of that could shape the future of our nation, help it, guide it the way it should go, the chances are that you could not get it on the air nor could you sustain it, because that type of visual imagery does not appeal to Aunt Maude in Peoria. Unfor-

> "
>
> In 1968, Gene Roddenberry, worried the network axe would prevent the Enterprise from completing her five year mission, made a promise to NBC
>
> "

tunately, science fiction fans are the lousiest audience in the world; they think, which is heresy! If we have every fan in the country gathered to us and it would be an audience of seven or eight million people; an audience that would honor the creators of any show, we would go off the air after fifteen episodes."

Roddenberry paused for a moment before continuing. "It is one of the unfortunate curses of television," he insisted. "You can have as high as eleven or twelve million devoted fans, more people than have seen Shakespeare since the beginning, and be a failure because at a certain time on a certain night you have to pass the magic number of fourteen million. At any rate, you [via the letter writing campaign] scared the hell out of the network, and they decided to keep the show on.

"At that time," Roddenberry elaborated, "I was committed to then produce the show, personally oversee every aspect of it. About ten days later, I received a phone call at breakfast and the network executive said, 'Hello, Gene Baby...' Well, I knew I was in trouble right then. He said, 'We have had a group of statistical experts researching your audience, researching youth and youth-oriented people, and we don't want you on a weeknight at an early time. We have picked the best youth spot that there is. All of our research confirms this, and it's great for the kids and that time is 10:00 on Friday nights.' I said, 'No doubt that is why you had the great kiddie show **The Bell Telephone Hour** on there last year.'

"Well, I want you to understand some of the politicking, some of the pressures they dropped on me. The only gun I then had was to stand by my original commitment, that I would not personally produce the show unless they returned us to the weeknight time they promised. As a matter of fact, I threatened for a time to walk with the whole show, because this was the only possible muscle—I don't own General Motors or anything like that — so I had to threaten them with the one thing I do on the show, which is what I might be able to bring to the show on a lone producership level. I wasn't particularly anxious to put in a third year of fourteen hours a day, six days a week, but **Star Trek** was my baby, and I was willing to risk it if I could have a reasonable shot at a reasonable time. And we talked it over and held fast. We almost swayed them and ultimately they said, 'No, we will not do it.' And then I had no option. I could not then say, 'Well, I'll produce it anyway,' because from then on with the network any threat or promise or anything I made ... once you back down, you

> **"**
>
> I had to threaten them with the one thing I do on the show.
>
> **"**

16

become the coward and your muscle from then on in any subsequent projects will never mean anything. So I had no option but to drop back and become executive producer of the show, and I did find a producer, Fred Freiberger."

Issue number 39 of *Starlog Magazine*, published in October of 1980, featured a piece in which Freiberger defended his efforts for **Star Trek** by stating that the ratings of the show were pretty much the same during all three seasons. There simply was not a large enough television audience to successfully continue the series.

"**Star Trek** became the legend it's become when it went into syndication," he pointed out. "The problem I was facing was how to broaden the viewer base. Do a science fiction show, but get enough additional viewers to keep the show on the air. I decided to do what I would hope was a broad canvas of shows, but I tried to make them more dramatic and to do stories that had more conventional storylines within the science fiction frame. Now if some science fiction fans didn't like it because it went too dramatic ... I'm guilty. That was deliberate."

Margaret Armen, who has written for seasons two and three of the series, as well as the animated version and the proposed sequel show, relates her feelings on the differences between Roddenberry and Freiberger.

"Fred came in and to him **Star Trek** was 'tits in space,' " she says. "That's a direct quote. I was in the projection room seeing an early episode when Fred came in and watched it with me and said, 'Oh, I get it. Tits in space.' Fred was looking for all action pieces, whereas Gene was looking for the subtlety that is **Star Trek**. Action, but with people carrying the story."

While season three is often dismissed by fans, who cite such episodes as "Spock's Brain" and "The Way to Eden" as "inappropriate," there were some fine shows produced, including "The Tholian Web," "The Paradise Syndrome," "Day of the Dove" and "All Our Yesterdays." Unfortunately, the show never improved in the ratings and was finally cancelled, with no hope of a second letter writing campaign changing NBC's corporate mind.

66

Fred came in and to him **Star Trek** was 'tits in space.'

99

And so, **Star Trek** came to an end, but as history has shown, in actuality it was only the beginning. **17**

Syndication has been known to turn many a show into a sensation, with independent stations "stripping" the series five nights a week and giving viewers a daily dose of what they find most appealing. It is in syndication that Ralph Kramden continues to threaten Alice with a free trip to the moon for over three decades; in which Lucy digs herself out of one mess and right into another; and which perpetuates the ongoing sloppy versus neat conflict of Oscar and Felix. It has already allowed the starship Enterprise to not only complete its five-year mission but continue its voyages for another eighteen.

Star Trek scored such a ratings disappointment for NBC, that the final episode, "Turnabout Intruder," never aired in prime time. It showed up instead when the series began its syndicated run. In the fall of 1970, Paramount began offering the show to independents, hoping that they would be able to recoup a few lost dollars on this "dog." Despite a slow beginning, the number of stations interested in carrying the series gradually increased, with the audience, in turn, growing as well.

Shortly thereafter, it became obvious that something was brewing. With Neil Armstrong's boot gracing the lunar surface the previous July, outer space suddenly became in vogue. Space was the place, and **Star Trek** was the ticket to get there.

"**Star Trek** probably came along too early," explained Gene Roddenberry in *The Making of Star Trek: The Motion Picture* [1980, Wallaby Books]. "Had man landed on the moon during our first or second year, the idea of space flight wouldn't have seemed so ludicrous to the mass audience. **Star Trek** probably would have stayed on the air. The eye of the world did not turn to space seriously as a future possibility until we were in our third year, and by then it was too late.

"In the last ten years, the future has suddenly come upon us. People are beginning to realize that the future is happening now. Whereas ten or fifteen years ago the future was something a quarter century or half century ahead, the rate of human development is moving so fast now that the future has finally caught up with us. Today you can't risk not thinking about the future, because many of the things you take for granted today may not even be here tomorrow."

With the continually mounting interest in **Star Trek** came the idea of a convention dedicated to the show, which would be held

> **"**
>
> **Star Trek** probably came along too early. Had man landed on the moon during our first or second year, the idea of space flight wouldn't have seemed so ludicrous to the mass audience.
>
> **"**

19

in New York during January of 1972. Episodes would be shown, merchandise pertaining to the series sold, and fans given the opportunity to meet and listen to the creative talents behind the series. The promoters of the con were expecting, with a little luck, maybe two or three hundred people. They were not prepared for the two thousand that actually showed up.

A year later, a second convention was held, with guests including James Doohan, George Takei, and Trek and science fiction writer David Gerrold. Again the promoters took what they thought would be adequate precautions, and again they were wrong. This time between six and seven thousand fans showed up. The same thing happened in 1974 when what is estimated to be between ten and fourteen thousand people attended. A firmer grip was placed on crowd control for the 1975 convention when registration was closed at approximately eight thousand. Those people lucky enough to get in, experienced William Shatner's first (and now all too rare) con appearance. The next year's convention was limited to six thousand people, and guests included DeForest Kelley, Gene Roddenberry, Majel Barrett, James Doohan, Nichelle Nichols and George Takei.

"The first convention had been the only hint that something was happening," explains David Gerrold, whose book, *The World of Star Trek*, explored the entire phenomenon, and helped, to some degree, in expanding it. "Then they were going to do one in '73, which I went to, and six thousand people showed up. That was the first real hint that this thing was not dead. But the studio said, 'Three thousand people is no big thing.' You really needed to demonstrate a continuing phenomenon, which had not been demonstrated at that time. So my book was out there, and here were all these fans who did not know that other fans existed. But every fan who got the book, got a list of fan clubs and things like that, and every fan found out about other fans. We kept the fan club and convention list updated so that by the time things [the conventions] started to peter out, we noticed that an incredible network of fans had been created. I don't take credit for all of it, but I claim credit for triggering a large part of it, because I also helped the other conventions build up their lists. Once the process was initiated, it became a chain reaction, and towards the end of '74 or '75, we began to notice that the phenomenon had developed into something really big."

Throughout the "convention years," the syndicated episodes were breaking all kinds of records, easily equalling itself the most pop-

> "
>
> Once the process was initiated, it became a chain reaction, and towards the end of '74 or '75, we began to notice that the phenomenon had developed into something really big.
>
> "

ular shows in reruns, including **I Love Lucy** and **The Honey-mooners**. Paramount noted this with interest, and was somewhat more than intrigued when the public began to demand a revival of the show. Rumors abounded, with the general feeling being that **Star Trek** would either come back as a new television series or perhaps even a feature film.

Still, Paramount made no official move. It's likely that they viewed the phenomenon as little more than a passing fad; that any such revival would, in effect, "miss the boat," and they would stand to lose even more money.

.They were wrong. **Star Trek** was no fad.

While fandom flourished, as did the merchandising of the show, animation production companies began to approach Gene Roddenberry and Paramount Pictures with the hope of securing the rights to do an animated version. Many of these suggestions were turned down, but Filmation came to them with a package that they liked. The idea was to do a series that would air on Saturday mornings, but would also feature the basic ideals of the original show. Both Roddenberry and Paramount agreed that this would be a good idea, and to that end the original cast was signed to provide the voices for their animated counterparts. Many of the writers involved with the live-action series also returned to pen scripts. Former **Star Trek** story editor, Dorothy Fontana, was signed to repeat her duties for the animated series, and to take on new ones as associate producer.

By the time the animated **Star Trek** had come along, Gene Roddenberry had created a pair of pilots which had not gone to series, **The Questor Tapes** and **Genesis II**. The former dealt with an android (Robert Foxworth) seeking to understand the human equation (which, ironically, would be the premise behind the character of Data on the later **Star Trek: The Next Generation** series). The latter chronicled the attempts of 20th Century researcher Dylan Hunt and the PAX scientific team of the future to rebuild Earth after an apocalyptic war.

"I was Gene's assistant on **The Questor Tapes**," says Fontana, "but didn't have anything to do with writing it. I knew of it from beginning to end, and thought it was a darn good show that could have gone to series. Unfortunately, Universal decided not to go with it. I thought that it had the makings of a show that could touch the audience in the way that **Star Trek** did.

> "
>
> Paramount made no official move. ...they viewed the phenomenon as little more than a passing fad; that any such revival would, in effect, "miss the boat," and they would stand to lose even more money. They were wrong. **Star Trek** was no fad
>
> "

21

"I had written a script for Genesis II, but it never got produced. The way that Gene wrote the original TV movie, it had potential to become a successful series, but not as seen in the last two movies [reformatted and titled Planet Earth]. It had been changed around an awful lot, but not for the better, although Gene did the first change himself."

The animated **Star Trek** series followed.

"When Gene approached me to do the show," she explains, "he asked me if I would like to come on as story editor and producer. Since I wasn't a part of another regular staff at the time, I decided to do it. I had not worked in animation, which I do enjoy, so I had a good time on the show. I left after the first season, because I wanted to move on to something else and not get stuck in animation. The business is funny. If you stay too long in one thing, people start to buttonhole you there and say, 'You can't do anything else,' regardless of all your other credits."

Twenty-two episodes were produced in all, and, for the most part, Fontana's efforts in securing the finest possible talent paid off. Those scripts, penned by Fontana herself as well as veterans from the old show and the genre, proved themselves to be quite literate, a bright spot on the Saturday morning schedule. Unfortunately, like its predecessor, **Star Trek Animated** was cancelled prematurely.

> **"**
>
> I had not worked in animation, which I do enjoy, so I had a good time on the show.
>
> **"**

Star Trek now had two strikes against it, but also a fan following which wouldn't let it die.

During the early seventies," explains David Gerrold, "NBC was the villain, because they had cancelled **Star Trek**, and Gene made sure that everybody knew that NBC was the villain. Gene was this man who wanted to change the world for the better, and NBC wouldn't let him. Then the movement shifted to, 'Gee, let's have a **Star Trek** movie,' and all of a sudden Paramount is the bad guy. It was always NBC was the villain for the series and Paramount was the villain for the movies, and it wasn't that way.

"By 1977," he continues, "some of the fans were beginning to perceive that Gene was the reason for the delay in the **Star Trek** movies, because the word did get out that he hadn't come to terms on his contract, and while some of the fans were mad at Gene, for the most part the public perception was, and Gene was carefully nurturing it ... he'd go out to various speaking engagements and he would say, 'It's difficult. How do you convince the studio executives that what you're talking about is changing the world?' And he'd do it very slyly. We're talking about studio executives, who are maligned by everyone who works for them. If a studio makes fifteen hit pictures in a year, who gets the credit? The directors, the actors, the executive producers of the picture. But the studio executive who said, 'I'll buy this picture, I'll finance it,' —he's 'just lucky enough to be sitting there when they brought the project in to him.'

"I have to tell you that I've spent a lot of time with studio executives, and they can tell the difference between a good story and a bad story. They get excited when they work with exciting people. You don't get to be the head of a studio by accident, and the ones I've met are not stupid men. Admittedly there have been some stupid men as studio executives who do make mistakes, but twenty years at Paramount? Paramount is the most successful studio in the industry. Down the line they're doing all these great pictures like **The Godfathers**, **Saturday Night Fever** ... and they can't get **Star Trek** on the boards? Give me a break."

Whether this assessment is correct or not, one cannot deny the fact that *something* was causing this project innumerable delays. In any case, Roddenberry was given his old office at the studio and told to write a movie script for a low-budget feature film.

"They turned me down a couple of times," Roddenberry said some nine years ago, "then finally they said, 'Write a script and we'll give you an office on the lot and think about it.' They were

> **"**
> It was always NBC was the villain for the series and Paramount was the villain for the movies, and it wasn't that way.
> **"**

23

23RD CENTURY EARTH CONTEXT FOR ENTERPRISE CREW BY JON POVILL

If the optimistic vision of the future that **Star Trek** traditionally depicts is to have a feeling of genuine reality, it is necessary that our characters reflect attitudes that are more highly evolved than those of normal contemporary dramas.

Consider: most people today who consider mankind's problems as insurmountable, base their assumption on the notion of human nature being

24

not that serious about [it] when we first started. I think they had in mind a $2-$3 million picture."

"I was working on the series **Barbary Coast**," explained actor William Shatner, forever known as Captain James T. Kirk, "which was done at Paramount. It was on one end of Paramount, and **Star Trek** had been filmed at the other end of Paramount. I had not, for the longest time, revisited the stage area where [we had] filmed. So one day I decided to go there, [and] as I'd been walking and remembering the times, I suddenly heard the sound of a typewriter! That was the strangest thing, 'cause these offices were deserted. So I followed the sound, 'till I came to the entrance of this building. And the sound was getting louder as I went into the building. I went down a hallway, where the offices for **Star Trek** were ... I opened the door and there was Gene Roddenberry! He was sitting in a corner, typing. I hadn't seen him in five years. I said, 'Gene, the series has been cancelled!' He said, 'I know, I know the series has been cancelled. I'm writing the movie!' So I said, 'There's gonna be a movie? What's it gonna be about?' He said, 'First of all, we have to explain how you guys got older. So what we have to do is move everybody up a rank. You become an Admiral, and the rest of the cast become Starfleet commanders. One day a force comes toward Earth— might be God, might be the devil — breaking everything in its path, except the minds of the starship commanders. So we gotta find all the original crewmen for the starship Enterprise, but first—where is Spock? He's back on Vulcan, doing R&R; five year mission—seven years of R&R. He swam back upstream. So we gotta go get him.' I call that show 'What Makes Salmon Run?' So we get Spock, do battle and it was a great story, but the studio turned it down."

Although little is known about the resulting script, entitled "The God Thing," reports have stated that the premise questioned the very nature of God and the universe around us. Paramount was apparently not interested in a script which, essentially, pit Captain Kirk against God.

Director Richard Colla, who had helmed **The Questor Tapes** telemovie pilot, was very familiar with that particular screenplay, and recalls it fondly.

"That script was much more daring," he recalls. "They went off in search of that thing from outer space that was effecting everything. By the time they got on to the spaceship and got into its [the alien's] presence, it manifested itself and said, 'Do you know me?' Kirk said, 'No, I don't know who you are.' It said, 'Strange, how could you not know who I am?' So it shift-changed and became another image and said, 'Do you know me.' Kirk said, 'No, who are you?' It replied, 'The time has passed, and you should know me by now.' It shifts shapes again, and comes up in the form of Christ the Carpenter, and says, 'Do you know me?' And Kirk said, 'Oh, now I know who you are.' And he says, 'How strange you didn't know these other forms of me.' Really, what Gene had written was that this 'thing' was sent forth to lay down the law; to communicate the law of the universe, and that as time goes on the law needs to be reinterpreted. And at that time 2,000 years ago, the law was interpreted by this Carpenter image. As time went on, the law was meant to be reinterpreted, and the Christ figure was meant to reappear in different forms. But this machine malfunctioned, and it was like a phonograph record that got caught in a groove, and kept grooving back, grooving back, grooving back. It's important to understand the essence of all this and reinterpret it as time goes on. That was a little heavy for Paramount. It was meant to be strong and moving, and I'm sorry it never got made."

"I handed them a script and they turned it down," Roddenberry stated matter-of-factly in 1980. "It was too controversial. It talked about concepts like, 'Who is God?' [In it] the Enterprise meets God in space; God is a life form, and I wanted to suggest that there may have been, at one time in the human beginning, an alien entity that early man believed was God, and kept those legends. But I also wanted to suggest that it might have been as much the Devil as it was God. After all, what kind of god would throw humans out of Paradise for eating the fruit of the Tree of Knowledge? One of the Vulcans on board, in a very logical way, says, 'If this is your God, he's not very impressive. He's got so many psychological problems; he's so insecure. He demands worship every seven days. He goes out and creates faulty humans and then blames them for his own mistakes. He's a pretty poor excuse for a Supreme Being.' Not surprisingly, that didn't send the Paramount executives off crying with glee. But I think good science fiction, historically, has been used that way—to question *everything*.

"[Anyway,] the movie then sagged for quite some time," he continued. "It really got bogged down. I didn't hear anything for over three months. Meanwhile, unknown to me, the executives then in charge were interviewing writers, accepting outlines. I found out about all this quite by accident. None of the outlines

greedy, corrupted, and fear-ridden. Rightly, they claim that this planet is quite capable of providing for our needs, but that man, jealous and possessive, is insatiable—and will remain that way till the end, even if it means his destruction.

Seeing as how **Star Trek** presumes that man did not destroy himself, we can expect to see some ways in which human nature no longer is quite as plagued by these negative aspects. After all, we really won't make it to the **Star Trek** century if these changes don't occur.

This does not necessarily mean that our people must be paragons of virtue, but it does mean that they must be *aware!* Unless such behavior is being caused by strange phenomenon, we must not see our characters motivated by common 20th Century frailties.

For example: These men and women have little interest in possessions, be they things or lovers. If they do possess some-

25

thing, it is likely to be with the attitude of an appreciative collector—ready to share with those of similar proclivities—rather than a jealously guarded hoarder.

These people are turned on and curious about the unknown, rather than fearful of it. They expect danger. They joined Starfleet at least in part because of the challenge that uncharted space provides. They will generally hit peak operating efficiency in a crisis rather than fold under the pressure of it.

Normally there would be no evidence of ego problems in our characters. They presumably were reared with more love and greater skills than most of us and so have grown up without most of the difficulties and defensiveness that we are heir to.

They are not ashamed of their bodies or bodily functions. These are people who can share bathroom facilities without regard for gender and

were accepted. I think the main reason for all the problems with those scripts rested in the fact that most of the people making decisions concerning the film knew little or nothing about **Star Trek**. As it turned out later on, several of the principals had never even seen the show."

Despite this statement to the contrary, according to *The Making of Star Trek: The Motion Picture*, some script activity took place between Paramount's rejection of "The God Thing" and their soliciting story ideas from other writers.

Jon Povill, who would eventually go on to be story editor of the proposed **Star Trek II** television series and associate producer of the first film, had worked with Gene Roddenberry as a researcher for what was then planned to be a novelization of "The God Thing."

"Gene went to work on that script in May of 1975," details Povill, "and it was his first attempt at a **Star Trek** feature. By August it was discarded by [Paramount President] Barry Diller. Gene, who had gotten to know me pretty well by then, suggested that I take a crack at writing a treatment, which I did."

The resulting treatment dealt with the people of planet Vulcan going mad, and the Enterprise's mad-dash through time to set things right by combatting a psychic-cloud that is affecting the population.

"Gene read it," Povill recalls, "and said, 'It would make a nice episode, but it's not a feature.' But then in December he called me and said, 'I have another idea for a feature, would you like to come in and help me write the treatment?' In January I moved into my office and started working on the treatment."

To summarize the resulting treatment: A mass of pulsating crystal plasma contains the mangled, apparently lifeless bodies of Kirk and the Enterprise crew. Then the bodies heal, slowly disappear and rematerialize on the Enterprise. Kirk and company learn that the Enterprise had been studying a black hole when suddenly there was a surge of energy. The shuttle crew including Spock and Scotty is still missing.

Chekov announces that they've all been dead for eleven years and when they arrive on Earth, there is no sign of Starfleet Command.

Uhura locates the survivors of the shuttle mission. Kirk and Spock beam down to their wilderness habitat, and are informed that shortly after the scientists arrived, the planet's surface was suddenly covered with a vast, ugly urban sprawl, and the world was abruptly populated by a "race of mindless automatons who do nothing but eat, sleep and perform their designated functions within the social order." They ask about Scotty, and are told that he had been working in a special laboratory in Munich, studying the time gap. Scotty, they realize, is somehow the source of the time-shift that altered the universe.

The Enterprise travels backwards in time and they discover a replica of the laboratory they seek in Munich, commemorating the initial appearance of the "Mediator" in 1937. The Mediator brought peace and optimism to the world, cured diseases and fed the hungry. He can be found at the League of Nations headquarters in Geneva.

Scott's interference led the world to become slave to a computer. When his first experiments had proved successful, five years later he attempted time travel to prevent the black hole incident. Something went wrong and he suddenly found himself surrounded by German soldiers. He used phasers to prevent World War II and developed potent medicines and agricultural systems to save lives and eliminate famine.

Kirk tells Scotty about the future and Scotty explains that he could use his knowledge to alter even that. Spock disagrees.

Everyone but Scotty beams back aboard the Enterprise to begin their journey into the past to restore history. Unfortunately, Enterprise's engines will only take them back as far as 1940. Phasers lash out and destroy specified targets in both Geneva and Munich. A moment later, the Enterprise itself explodes.

A younger and happier Kirk, Spock and Scott appear at Starfleet Command in the proper time frame of the 23rd Century. Spock informs the Command Officer that his time gap calculations were mistaken, and investigation of the black hole will not be necessary.

The Enterprise crew has been rewarded by the plasma entity— actually the evolved form of humanity in the alternate future— with another chance at life.(For a more detailed explanation of this script please see the Appendix under "Star Trek II.")

This scenario was certainly an interesting one, and, if developed properly, would have made a terrific feature film debut for **Star Trek**.

without embarrassment. Nor would it cause any awkwardness if someone were to interrupt a couple in the midst of love-making.

Relationships between the sexes are generally non-exclusive unless "contract marriage" is agreed upon, in which the two partners devote whatever portion of their lives that they wish to an exclusive arrangement for mutual growth, exploration and understanding. The contracts are renewable, which makes monogamy a possibility if it is a continued desire of both parties.

Earth Itself: The lifestyles and activities of 23rd Century Earth provide the social context of which our characters are supposed to have grown. But what are they? How do people occupy their time in a world that has solved the problems of hunger, disease, war and fear?

In our own time, we see that once people have attained a satisfactory level of material se-

27

curity, they begin to turn their attention to the question of personal fulfillment. Thus we may suspect that the primary pursuits of the 23rd Century are of personal growth, learning and awareness.

Diversity is a key. To 23rd Century humanity, diversity is welcomed as the provider of fresh stimuli from which one can learn and grow. The differences between people are sources of delight rather than threat.

Competition is welcomed as a means of stretching one's abilities. Sports and games are played with the true Olympian ideal in mind of excellence for its own sake rather than the notion of beating down one's opponent.

The arts flourish. Nearly everyone is involved in some sort of artistic endeavor. Most people can play a variety of traditional and exotic musical instruments. The demand for new instruments from alien cultures is, no doubt, high. There is live and holographic theatre,

In April of 1976, Povill expressed his thoughts concerning this treatment, giving every indication that a tremendous amount of thought had gone into its development, and providing insight to its meaning.

"Does the advancement of a technological civilization require that mankind must or will sublimate and subjugate pleasures into extinction?" he asked. "Is Captain Kirk, whose love is reserved for his inanimate ship, evolving into a Spock-like creature whose potential for love was extinguished in childhood by inanimate logic and order? Will the battle in a man's mind to retain his humanity grow more intense as the centuries advance? Will the human race build itself into a joyless condition, as the Vulcans did? Finally, the point relating to our story, where are the forks in such an evolutionary road and what are the future prospects of man along each route?

"Plot connection," Povill continued. "If the crystal-plasma body at the beginning of the script was, in fact, a future incarnation of the human race, something that mankind evolved into, which, for all its awesome power lacked any aspect of joy, might not it use its power to try to recapture joy if possible? If Scotty's presence in the 20th Century preempted the humanistic revolution of the late sixties through the present by solving problems through purely technical means, then by the 29th Century mankind might well evolve into a vaguely dissatisfied blob of all-powerful crystal plasma.

"The 23rd or 24th Century Earth that the ship returns to might be well on its way to that condition. I think it is safe to assume that Scotty's interference in the 20th Century would produce, by the 23rd Century, a world that was vastly superior to the Earth Kirk knows. The inhabitants would at the same time be totally devoid of emotion, or, like Spock, be tortured by emotions which can find no outlet through the intellectual trap. These beings would also be thoroughly convinced that they were on the right track. After all, there have been no wars, poverty or strife since Scotty's time (the 20th Century). Perhaps there are camps where less evolved emotional, human types are humanely detained 'for their own safety.'

"Coming home to an Earth of this nature would be an even more difficult problem for Kirk and company than the return in the earlier version. There would be the danger of internment in the 'less evolved' camps. The odds would be more highly stacked against our heroes in any interactions they undertake with the more evolved Earth beings. In addition, we would have the *clear* dilemma that these people are *at once superior and inferior* to mankind as we know it. Kirk's later actions will then be more apparent as *opting* for *humanity* and *emotion* rather than simply the vague intellectual principal that things must proceed along the given lines of history, though that point will still be implicit. The import of Kirk's direction can perhaps be verified by some sign at the end that the crystal-plasma entity has, or will, achieve satisfaction.

"This set-up holds an additional advantage," Povill added. "By making the 23rd Century clearly superior yet distinctly distasteful, our audience will be rooting for World War II to be fought. Too many people would find our early image of a Century-Citified Earth quite acceptable and not enough of a loss to require suffering to change. We need the audience to *want* the chance to fight the damned wars and solve the problems on our own as they come up. We are reaffirming humanity, not philosophy, and this should be clear enough to get the audience with us on this point early on. Make them *want* to throw off the unbridled progress. This is no less dramatic than having them feel ambivalent about throwing away an advanced 1970.

"Corollary plot notes," he concluded on the subject. "It might be fitting and helpful to the plot and an audience unfamiliar with **Star Trek** if, after the crew was revived, they found themselves in the throes of an identity crisis. Who are they, what are they doing out in space, what are their real wants and needs? I would like to see some 23rd Century psychology applied—really advanced adjustment techniques. Perhaps a machine that takes people back to their childhoods or other appropriate moments of crisis or decision. On a screen we might see some formative moments of important crew members as they tried to readjust to their situation. Also, perhaps a group session to reaffirm for the crew and establish for the audience closer emotional ties amongst them than we have yet seen. [This] would certainly be in keeping with a rebirth and could be a dramatic crisis as well if it were thought that the crystal plasma was messing up the crew's minds as some sort of weapon to keep the Enterprise from effectively combatting the influence that the entity exerts over them early on. It would later be apparent that the crystal-plasma was merely trying to return them to the roots of their humanity as part of the mission being undertaken."

mime and dance, all in traditional styles as well as newer, more exotic and more highly athletic modes. These activities are all participant (as opposed to purely spectator) oriented.

Appearance of the Planet: If we have the opportunity to see Earth, we will discover that it has been largely returned to its natural state. Lush forests and barren deserts are preserved in pollution-free purity. Industry, commerce and transportation facilities are predominantly underground so that the surface of the planet can be a place to be enjoyed.

In some cases, old cities have been refurbished and are maintained in mint condition so that those who wish to may have the pleasure of riding a San Francisco cable car or taking a stroll through Soho, as their ancestors did centuries before.

There are totally automated farms, but there are also farms

that are run entirely by people who wish the joy of cultivating the land.

What was once the state of Kansas has been made a Plains Indian lifestyle area in which people of any race can live and hunt as the Plains Indians did. There are other such areas accommodating nearly every culture from the past so that people can truly know what these existences were like (it should be mentioned that in these areas, technology is not permitted to soften the experience. The "tribe," or whatever, is every bit as much in the hands of nature as the society it recreates).

There are cities of huge bamboo and tree pole architecture in Africa that have been preserved from the 21st Century African Renaissance.

There are prehistoric parks, for which genetic engineering has provided living, breeding reproductions of many long extinct species of reptiles, mammals and birds.

Apparently these notes struck a chord with Gene Roddenberry, as two days later he issued his own concerning the treatment and where he would like to see the proposed script go.

"We probably should say that the architecture may look somewhat advanced plus neat and clean to our film audience, but that it seems very primitive to our 23rd Century characters," Roddenberry pointed out in referring to the first beam down to Earth in the future. "This leads to the interesting question of why there have been no architectural advances in the last several centuries. In other words, it is our first indication that this quality of *total* peace and order has taken away humankind's bruises, disappointments, angers and frustrations which lead to all the dissatisfactions and torments which cause people to rebel against present things and create better things.

"The people are no longer capable of *original* thought," he elaborated. "They can think, perhaps even efficiently, within their areas of specialization, but are simply totally lost outside that area. [Yet] every physical need is taken care of; he has absolutely no wants!

"McCoy, always our humanitarian, can argue that it comes pretty close to being the best of all possible worlds. Who's to say that their own rather anarchial 23rd Century society is any better? These people are never threatened in any way, never lied to, all of their senses are regularly gratified. They may not develop intimate personal relationships like us, but they do have a marvelous sense of being an integral and protected part of the whole socio-organism which they deeply and sincerely love. The socio-organism, in fact, fulfills one of humankind's most ancient needs, i.e., to be fully and firmly a part of something bigger than the human's selfish self.

"Couldn't the Enforcers [police officers of this altered future] carry phasers? Scotty no doubt had a phaser when he went back in time. Perhaps he's added to it a 'pleasure' setting which sends the victim into positive throes of ecstasy before, at the height of 'orgasm,' being eliminated. It could be argued that the orgasm seems to the victim to last a hundred years or so. Before being eliminated, they seem to themselves to actually live an incredibly pleasant 'lifetime' before dying for the good of the socio-organism. Hell, who's going to worry about *that* kind of death? Maybe *all* deaths at the end of a usefully productive life are arranged this way. Sort of something to look forward to. Hell, you can't get people to rebel against *that*!

"By the time Kirk gets to discussing the situation and making the decision, he should be a troubled man," added Roddenberry. "I said something in the rewrite I gave you about someone criticizing the fact he is 'playing God' by going back and changing history all over again. Kirk is a bright man raised in the philosophy of IDIC and this has got to cause him considerable utter turmoil.

"As we discussed earlier, the crystal-plasma mass sent some kind of a message to Kirk which was so powerful it damned near shorted out his mind. All he could get out of it was a sort of feeling of loneliness. Is it possible that Spock, using mind-meld, might try to use his own brain to determine whether or not there was an intelligent life form's message? If so, Spock might volunteer to attempt to try to decipher that message. It is possible the message could be so complex that even Spock isn't able to come right out with it. Perhaps it takes weeks of Vulcan meditation. During these weeks, the Enterprise could have gone back in time, still not having made the decision whether to interfere. We do have a nice 'will he or won't he?' question hanging over our story for a while. Maybe the temporary decision is that they'll go back to the earlier century and if they decide not to interfere, they'll simply live there since it is at least a world somewhat closer to their own. But at the last moment, Spock finally understands the message.

"Since I am smarter than Spock," he joked, "and *know* what the crystal-plasma mass said, here it is: It is in fact humankind's future to become a 'oneness' with itself and indeed with the entire universe. But it is the plan of the universe for this to happen to intelligent life forms eons later. It has happened to humankind long before they are ready. In short, they've found a 'oneness' in themselves without finding it with the universe. As such, they blundered into the ultimate selfishness. The crystal-plasma mass is condemned to live separately from all the rest of the universe through all time. Hence the loneliness.

"I hope to God you can say the above in a simpler way," he closed. "I guess what *I* am actually trying to say is that our destiny is to become a part of God, which is really All. Because changed humanity was not allowed to grow through adolescence and adulthood in the normal fashion, it never made the All. Individualism, *selfish* individualism, is absolutely necessary. When the time comes for that to be changed, it will happen of itself. But humankind *must* live through the entire stage and extract every

There are "art cities" planned, designed and built by artists, sculptors and architects as ongoing showcases that constantly change.

In short, Earth has become a world that is at once a playground and a living library. A place where people can feel free to experience whatever activities they want for the sake of their own chosen development as individuals. And if one's personality demands even greater stimulation than all this provides, there is always "Space, the final frontier...", which tells us a lot about the people who crew the starship Enterprise.

31

bit of knowledge and experience from it before moving on to a higher plateau of existence."

Pretty thought-provoking stuff.

Needless to say, this story was rejected as well, and **Star Trek** was back at ground zero.

The studio's search for the proper vehicle to launch the first **Star Trek** film began around this time. The writers approached included John D.F. Black, who had served as story editor of the original show's first season and penned "The Naked Time," and then wrote the story for the "Justice" episode of the new series; famed author Harlan Ellison, whose sole contribution to the show had been its most popular episode, "City on the Edge of Forever," and science fiction veteran Robert Silverberg.

John D.F. Black describes the storyline he pitched with a good-natured shrug. Something in his voice conveys the feeling that he still can't believe the way the studio handled the proposed film.

"I came up with a story concept involving a black hole," recounts Black, "and this was *before* Disney's film. The black hole had been used by several planets in a given constellation as a garbage dump. But with a black hole there's a point of equality. In other words, when enough positive matter comes into contact with an equal amount of negative matter, the damn thing blows up. Well, if that ever occurs with a black hole, it's the end of the universe—it'll swallow everything. What I saw was that the Enterprise discovered what's happened with this particular black hole and they try to stop these planets from unloading into it. The planets won't do it. It comes to war in some areas and, as a result, the black hole comes to balance and blows up. At that point, it would continue to chew up matter. In one hundred and six years Earth would be swallowed by this black hole, and the Enterprise is trying to beat the end of the world. There were at least twenty sequels in that story because the jeopardy keeps growing more intense."

Paramount rejected the idea. "They said it wasn't big enough," Black notes wryly.

In his excellent nonfiction assessment of horror and science fiction, *Danse Macabre*, Stephen King reported that rumor had Harlan Ellison going to Paramount with the idea of the Enterprise breaking through the end of the universe and confronting God himself. And that wasn't big enough either.

Removing tongue from cheek, the author explained the real story to King, but before discussing that, it's important to note what writer James Van Hise wrote in his fanzine, **Enterprise Incidents**.

> " In one hundred and six years Earth would be swallowed by this black hole, and the Enterprise is trying to beat the end of the world. They said it wasn't big enough. "

It involved going to the end of the known universe to slip back through time to the Pleistocene period when man first emerged.

"The story Harlan came up with," Van Hise wrote in number eight of his magazine, "was never written down, but was presented verbally ... the story did not begin with any of the Enterprise crew, but started on Earth where strange phenomenon were inexplicably occurring. In India, a building where a family is having dinner, just vanishes into dust. In the United States, one of the Great Lakes suddenly vanishes, wrecking havoc. In a public square, a woman suddenly screams and falls to the pavement where she transforms into some sort of reptilian creature. The truth is suppressed, but the Federation realizes that someone or something is tampering with time and changing things on Earth in the far distant past. What is actually happening involves an alien race on the other end of the galaxy. Eons ago, Earth and this planet both developed races of humans and intelligent humanoid reptiles. On Earth, the humans destroyed the reptile men and flourished. In the time of the Enterprise when this race learns what happened on Earth in the remote past, they decide to change things in the past so that they will have a kindred planet. For whatever reason, the Federation decides that only the Enterprise and her crew are qualified for this mission, so a mysterious cloaked figure goes about kidnapping the old central crew. This figure is finally revealed to be Kirk. After they are reunited, they prepare for the mission into the past to save Earth. And that would have been just the first half hour of the film!"

Ellison gave Stephen King a little more information on his story meeting with Paramount.

"It involved going to the end of the known universe to slip back through time to the Pleistocene period when man first emerged," he said. "I postulated an alien intelligence from a far galaxy where the snakes had become the dominant life form, and a snake-creature who had come to Earth in the **Star Trek** feature, had seen its ancestors wiped out, and who had gone back into the far past of Earth to set up distortions in the time-flow so the reptiles could beat the humans. The Enterprise goes back to set time right, finds the snake-alien, and the human crew is confronted with the moral dilemma of whether it had the right to wipe out an entire life form just to insure its own territorial imperative in our present and future. The story, in short, spanned all of time and all of space, with a moral and ethical problem."

Paramount executive Barry Trabulus "listened to all this and sat silently for a few minutes," Ellison elaborated. "Then he said, 'You know, I was reading this book by a guy named Von Daniken and he proved that the Mayan calendar was exactly like ours, so it must have come from aliens. Could you put in some Mayans?'"

The writer pointed out that there were no Mayans at the dawn of time, but the executive brushed this off, pointing out that no one would know the difference.

"'I'm to know the difference,'" Ellison exploded.

"'It's a dumb suggestion.' So Trabulus got very uptight and said he liked Mayans a lot and why didn't I do it if I wanted to write this picture," Ellison continued. "So I said, 'I'm a writer. I don't know what the f—k you are!' And I got up and walked out. And that was the end of my association with the **Star Trek** movie."

The Robert Silverberg story, entitled **The Billion Year Voyage**, was more of an intellectual foray as the Enterprise crew discovered the ruins of an ancient, but far more advanced, civilization, and must battle other aliens in order to take possession of the wondrous gifts left behind; gifts which would surely benefit mankind some day in the future when he is ready to accept that responsibility.

> "
>
> So I said, 'I'm a writer. I don't know what the f—k you are!' And I got up and walked out.
>
> "

These three stories were fascinating attempts at reviving the show, and it seems unimaginable that all of them were turned down. The revival game was destined to continue for some time to come.

By 1976, **Star Trek** was celebrating its ten year anniversary, and the show's fan following was continuously growing larger, with the demand for a new film or television series growing more vehement. It had been seven years since the last new episode, and the only difference between then and now was that the idea of reviving the show, in one format or another, was actually being considered by Paramount.

At the same time, America was preparing for the next phase of its exploration of the final frontier: the space shuttle. This was the year that the orbiter would lift off into space via rocket boosters, and land like a plane. But first, there was the matter of the experimental model, which was designed to test the landing procedures, but not actually fly. The fans of **Star Trek** deluged President Gerald Ford with letters, and it was only a short matter of time before the President of the United States made the official announcement: this particular shuttle would have the name *Enterprise*, after the starship from the famed television series and continuing a historic series of vessels beginning with a ship in the Continental Navy in the American Revolution. To help celebrate the occasion, Gene Roddenberry and the cast from the show were invited to play a part in the ceremony on September 17, in which the shuttle would be hauled out of its hanger for the first time.

"They rolled out the space shuttle *Enterprise*," Roddenberry recalled. "The military band marched out and the leader raised his baton. I was waiting for 'Stars and Stripes Forever' or 'America the Beautiful,' or something. Instead, they played the **Star Trek** theme. Twice. I had this funny feeling in my stomach, you know, like that was going just a little too far. People ask me, 'Aren't you proud about the space shuttle?' Well, sure. But this morning we were all feeling uncomfortable. There were senators, generals and politicians all around. And the band was playing the **Star Trek** theme. I thought to myself, 'Geez, these are the people who are running our country!'

"I must admit that when they first announced that the shuttle was going to be named after the Enterprise, I didn't completely approve. I was afraid that my friends at NASA and in the space industry would think that it was a shrewd publicity ploy for the movie. You know, everyone has this stereotyped idea about producers who wear Hawaiian shirts, smoke big cigars and do anything to see a few lines in print. And that's all untrue. It was

> **"**
>
> I was waiting for 'Stars and Stripes Forever' or 'America the Beautiful,' or something. Instead, they played the **Star Trek** theme. Twice.
>
> **"**

37

the **Star Trek** *fans* that started all this. They began a letter-writing campaign to the President. I completely disassociated myself from it. I would have preferred the shuttle not bear a military name like the Constitution or the Enterprise. I would have named it after a famous rocket scientist.

"But a friend of mine told me later that I was just too close to the whole project to see it for what it was. The role of the arts, he said, was changing. The very function of art today is to give people goals, to inspire them. And apparently the Enterprise has inspired a lot of people."

Indeed. So strong had **Star Trek**'s following grown, that the show truly became a part of the national social conscience, and Paramount was not oblivious to this fact. Despite Roddenberry's concerns that the naming of the shuttle after his starship would come across as a cheap, albeit inventive, advertising ploy, it didn't hurt the studio's enthusiasm to bring the Enterprise to the big screen. If any attempt to do so seemed likely to succeed, it was the one initiated in July of 1976. Jerry Isenberg was hired as producer, with Phil (**Invasion of the Body Snatchers**, **The Right Stuff**) Kaufman directing. Scripting were a pair of English writers named Alan Scott and Chris Bryant, whose credits included **Don't Look Now** and **Joseph Andrews**. Their experience in science fiction was non-existent, but what they lacked in knowledge, they made up for in enthusiasm, and a willingness to learn.

Kaufman, in particular, was thrilled with the prospect of being involved. "George Lucas is a good friend of mine," he had told one reporter. "He told me before he made **Star Wars** he'd made inquiries as to whether **Star Trek** was available to be bought. I thought George had a great thing going. When I was asked if I would be interested in doing **Star Trek**, well ... I felt I could go through the roof."

In addition to all of this, the original cast had essentially been signed to reprise their original roles, with the exception of Leonard Nimoy, who, at the time, had refused all interviews pertaining to **Star Trek**. William Shatner, however, had no problem in discussing the situation.

"Leonard Nimoy has a beef, and it's a legitimate one," Shatner said in 1976. "It's about the merchandising and it's something that irks me as well. Our faces appear on products all over the country, all over the world, and we've not really been compensated fairly for it. Right now Paramount wants Leonard, and Leo-

The role of the art...was changing. The very function of art today is to give people goals, to inspire them.

nard wants fair recompense. It's only reasonable that Paramount meet his demands. Something has happened here. Someone has made a lot of money from the show, and the people who were the show have seen very little of it. I think Leonard is totally in the right."

While Nimoy would eventually agree to do this attempt to resurrect **Star Trek**, the format would again be changed and he would, again, drop out. As time went on, it seemed as though the problems facing cast and crew were unending, and yet, despite all this, Roddenberry remained optimistic.

"I'm very pleased with the way the film is going," he enthused at the time. "We've just signed Phil Kaufman—who's done many fine films—to direct. Things really began to change around here when the studio shifted its power base and David Picker took charge. He put Jerry Isenberg in command of the film, and Jerry knows how to deal with the front office quite well. Once these men entered the picture, things began to move quite smoothly.

"It's taking more time than usual to come up with a good script, because we're faced with some unusual problems. This is not just another movie—this is **Star Trek**. A lot of people in the business have said to me, 'Hey, it should be easy to do the film. Just do an extended TV episode. You've done lots already, just do it again.' Well, I didn't want to do it that way. A movie is different from a TV show in a lot of ways. For one thing, the audience has made an investment in the film. They've shelled out money for the ticket, as well as for parking, babysitters, maybe dinner. They don't want to see a TV show on the screen. They're a captive audience and they want something special. It's like getting a book and finding out it's lousy. If you've been given it as a present, you figure, gee, since I got it for free, it's no big deal that it's bad. But if you've paid for it, you get a little pissed off.

"With the **Star Trek** script, we have defined personalities and really can't do anything contrary to the behavior patterns we've already established in the past. We're finding out that it's easier to work from scratch in terms of a storyline, but because all the details of the film are so well known already, it's getting harder and harder to come up with something new. I don't know what we'll finish with at this point, but I'm sure it will be a film that has a lot of entertainment value—action, adventure and a little comedy. I want a **2,001**."

While Nimoy would eventually agree to do this attempt to resurrect **Star Trek**, the format would again be changed and he would, again, drop out. As time went on, it seemed as though the problems facing cast and crew were unending, and yet, despite all this, Roddenberry remained optimistic.

39

Unfortunately, he didn't get it. It wasn't from a lack of trying. The Scott/Bryant screenplay opens with the Enterprise investigating a distress signal sent from the USS DaVinci. By the time they arrive in that quadrant of space, the other starship is gone. Suddenly, Kirk's brain is struck by electromagnetic waves, which results in erratic behavior and his commandeering a shuttlecraft. He pilots it towards an invisible planet and disappears. Three years later, Spock leads an expedition back to that area of space, and they discover what they believe to be the planet of the Titans, an ancient, but highly advanced race which had been thought extinct. Problem is that the planet is being drawn towards a black hole, and it becomes a race against time between the Federation and the Klingons, who are both interested in that particular world. The one who saves the planet will receive the fruits of their knowledge.

On the planet's surface, Spock discovers Kirk, who has been living there as a wild man. The captain is restored to normal in short order, and together they discover that the planet is actually populated by the evil Cygnans, a race which had destroyed the Titans. The story concluded with Kirk, in an effort to destroy the hostile Cygnans, ordering the Enterprise *into* the black hole. As Susan Sackett noted in *The Making of Star Trek: The Motion Picture*, "During the trip through the black hole, the Cygnans are destroyed and the Enterprise emerges in orbit around Earth. But it is Earth at the time of the Cro-Magnon man, the dawn of humanity. The ancient Titans, it would seem, were the men of the Enterprise."

Jon Povill, who had shifted into the background as Gene Roddenberry's assistant, noted the project with interest, though he wasn't convinced it was right for **Star Trek**'s debut on the movie screen.

"It was an interesting script in a certain sort of way," Povill explains. "It was not **Star Trek**. People would have gone to see it, and it would have done as well as we did with **Star Trek: The Motion Picture**, but it's just as well that it didn't get made. Chris and Alan even felt that it was something that wasn't quite successful. They didn't feel they had brought off a script that was just right. They didn't feel confident about it. Then Phil Kaufman decided that he wanted to take a run at the script. His treatment was, I think, worse than the script. Then the whole thing kind of fell apart."

"

It was an interesting script in a certain sort of way. It was not **Star Trek.**.

"

It's been over a decade since the Scott/Bryant script had been written, and while Alan Scott cannot recall the specifics of the storyline, he has no trouble remembering his involvement with the proposed film.

"Jerry Isenberg brought us into the project," says Scott. "He was going to be the producer at the time. We came out and met with him and Gene. We talked about it, and I think the only thing we agreed on at the time was that if they were going to make **Star Trek** as a motion picture, we should try and go forwards as if it were from the television series. Take it into another realm, if you like, into another dimension, and to that end we were talking quite excitedly about a distinguished film director and Phil Kaufman's name came up. We all thought that was a wonderful idea, and we met with him. Phil is a great enthusiast and very knowledgeable about science fiction, and we did a huge amount of reading. We must have read thirty science fiction books of various kinds. At that time we also had that guy from NASA, who was one of the advisors on the project, Jesco Von Puttkamer. He was at some of the meetings, and Gene was at all of the meetings.

"We were under instructions at the time," he adds, the passage of years unclouding a bit, "that they had no deal with William Shatner, so in fact the first story draft we did eliminated Captain Kirk. It was only a month or six weeks later when we were called and told that Kirk was now aboard and should be one of the lead characters. So all that work was wasted. At that time, Chris and I would sit in a room and talk about story ideas and notions, and talk them through with either Phil or Gene. Without any ill feelings on anyone's part, it became clear to us that there was a divergence of view as to how the movie should be made between Gene and Phil. I think Gene was quite right in sticking by not so much the specifics of **Star Trek**, but general ethics of it. I think Phil was more interested in exploring a wider range of science fiction stories, and yet nonetheless staying faithful to **Star Trek**. There was definitely a tugging on the two sides between them. One of the reasons it took us so long to come up with a story was because things like that would change. If we came up with some aspects that pleased Gene, they often didn't please Phil and vice-versa. We were kind of piggies in the middle."

It's pointed out that in many instances there was a similar situation between Roddenberry and director Robert Wise on **Star Trek: The Motion Picture**.

66

If they were going to make **Star Trek** as a motion picture, we should try and go forwards as if it were from the television series. Take it into another realm.

99

41

"I would imagine," he replies earnestly. "Eventually we got to a stage where we more or less didn't have a story that everybody could agree on, and we were in very short time of our delivery date. Chris and I decided that the best thing we could do was take all the information we had absorbed from everybody, sit down and hammer something out. In fact, we did a fifteen or twenty page story in a three day time period. I guess amendments were made to that in light of Gene and Phil's recommendations, but already we were at a stage by then that the thing was desperate if we were going to make the movie according to the schedule that was given to us. We made various amendments, we went to the studio with it and they turned it down.

"We never heard the reasons that it was turned down. I think other political things intervened, and I think the management at Paramount changed as well. I'm almost sure that at that time Michael Eisner came in and David Picker left, and I think that may have been as significant as anything else that may have happened. Our working relationship with Gene was very good and very friendly. In fact, we're still friends. Similarly with Phil. The only thing I can remember about the story itself is the ending, and I truly don't remember anything else but the ending. It involved primitive man on Earth, and I guess Spock or the crew of the Enterprise inadvertently introduced primitive man to the concept of fire. As they accelerated away, we realized that they were therefore giving birth to civilization as we know it. That's the only thing I can remember. I know a black hole was very important to the story. I guess it was through the black hole that they ended up in time warp."

Although there had been a slight feeling of intimidation at the outset, this quickly faded as the writing duo got further involved.

"I think as time wore on, we became less intimidated and much more absorbed in the **Star Trek** ethic," Scott concurs. "You can't work on that project with Gene and not become involved with it. The difficulty for us was trying to make, as it were, an exploded episode of **Star Trek** that had its own justifications in terms of the new scale that was available to it. Much of the show's charm was the fact that it dealt with big and bold ideas on a small budget, and of course the first thing that a movie would do, potentially, was match the budget and scale of the production to the boldness and vigor of the ideas. Of course we spent weeks looking at every episode of **Star Trek**, and I would guess that more or less every member of the cast came by and met us.

"We were surprised that it didn't go, because it seemed that it would. It was absolutely a 'go' picture. But it was a very exciting project to be involved with. I'm sorry it didn't work, because we would have enjoyed it even more if it had. We had a lot of fun and it was really an enjoyable time. I don't feel unhappy about it at all. It was just one of those deals that happens at studios from time to time that fall down the middle."

Phil Kaufman's reaction to the cancellation of the film was not quite so idealistic. "We were dealing with important things," he said. "Things that George [Lucas] has a smattering of in **Star Wars**. We were dealing a lot with Olaf Stapledon. There were chapters in **Last and First Men** that I was basing **Star Trek** on. That was my key thing. Gene and I disagreed on what the nature of a feature film really is. He was still bound by the things that he had been forced into by lack of money and by the fact that those times were not into science fiction the way they are now."

Perhaps most shocking to him was the feeling that Paramount canceled the film because of the success of **Star Wars**, which was released in May of 1977, and the belief that they had blown their opportunity at the box office. "They didn't even wait to see what **Star Wars** would do," Kaufman said incredulously. "I don't think they tried to understand what the phenomenon of **Star Trek** was."

"We considered the project for years," summed up then Paramount president Barry Diller. "We've done a number of treatments, scripts, and every time we'd say, 'This isn't good enough.' If we had just gone forward and *done* it, we might have done it quite well. In this case [the Scott/Bryant/Kaufman version], it was the script. We felt, frankly, that it was a little pretentious. We went to Gene Roddenberry and said: 'Look, you're the person who really understands **Star Trek**. We don't. But what we should probably do is return to the original context, a television series.' If you force it as a big 75 millimeter widescreen movie, you go directly against the concept. If you rip **Star Trek** off, you'll fail, because the people who like **Star Trek** don't just like it. They love it."

So, once again, the Enterprise's destiny was being charted towards the television screen, although no one had any idea that she would never complete the voyage.

Gene and I disagreed on what the nature of a feature film really is. He was still bound by the things that he had been forced into by lack of money.

And the Earth shook.

If it didn't, then it must have been a movement of damn near equal proportion to the fans of a little television series they had refused to let die. They had taken "control" of the show's destiny by generating an unprecedented amount of enthusiasm, resulting in a phenomenon whose closest relative was probably Beatlemania circa 1964. They gathered together at conventions, met their idols, penned original fiction dedicated to the characters and ideals of the show and never stopped hoping for the day when it would be resurrected on either television or the movie screen. In the middle of 1977, it seemed as though their efforts had finally borne fruit: **Star Trek** was returning to television.

After numerous attempts to bring the show back as either a feature film, television movie or weekly series, it finally seemed that a revival would come to pass. The original cast, with the exception of Leonard Nimoy, who for career and litigation reasons did not wish to reprise the role of Spock on a weekly basis, had actually been signed to play their most famous roles. Scripts were being developed and sets constructed for the brand new starship Enterprise. Everything was coming together, allowing **Star Trek** to touch a new generation in the same way it had the previous one.

For some time, Paramount Pictures had dreamed of starting a fourth network to compete with the three majors, much as the Dumont Network did during television's Golden Age. To this end, they contacted independent stations all over the United States and began offering product to fill one night a week with new programming, cornerstoned by the series entitled **Star Trek II**.

Robert Goodwin had been with Paramount Pictures for two years. Originally he was assistant to Arthur Fellows, who, in turn, was the Senior Vice President in charge of television production and had taken over Playboy Enterprises, whose name had been changed to Playboy-Paramount. Goodwin spent approximately one year there as the Director of Development.

"Then a guy named Gary Nardino came in and took over as President of Paramount Television, and made the decision to start a fourth network," Goodwin details. "The plan was that every Saturday night they were going to do one hour of **Star Trek** and then a two hour movie. My interest had always been more in the long form rather than the series side of television. Nardino decid-

> "
>
> For some time, Paramount Pictures had dreamed of starting a fourth network to compete with the three majors, much as the Dumont Network did during television's Golden Age. To this end, they contacted independent stations all over the United States and began offering product to fill one night a week with new programming, cornerstoned by the series entitled **Star Trek II**.
>
> "

45

ed that he was going to put me in charge of all these two hour movies, which was great for me."

At that point, forces were at work which would pull Goodwin away from this choice assignment and bring him over to Roddenberry's team. Meanwhile, Roddenberry himself grew more vibrant with each passing day, as a seven year battle to bring **Star Trek** back seemed at an end. He was essentially being given the opportunity to top himself, although he never really looked at it that way.

"Those [original] episodes will always be there for what people want to make out of them," he told *Starlog* at the time. "We're making a new set of them ten years later under very different circumstances. I think neither takes away from the other. The worst that can happen is someone would say that Roddenberry couldn't do it a second time. That doesn't bother me, as long as I did my damndest to do it a second time."

What was truly exciting to him was the opportunity to deal with different social issues in a new and fresh style, as television had been altered considerably by such series as **M*A*S*H** and **All in the Family**. Gone were the days when you *had* to hide your ideas within entertainment, for fear that network censors would not allow the show on the air. Things had changed to such a degree, that television was actually *challenged* to express itself in new and different ways.

"Dialogue is more naturalistic on television today," Roddenberry explained. "Direction is more sophisticated. There are better methods of optical effects. There are better methods for special effects. The audience is certainly more sophisticated and able to reach their minds out further. The audience is ready for statements on sex, religion, politics and so on, which we never would have dared to make before."

Star Trek II was envisioned as a dream come true, and efforts were made to secure the proper creative team. First choice was the aforementioned Robert Goodwin as producer.

"They were looking for someone to come on as producer," says Goodwin, "and Gene Roddenberry had heard about me. To be perfectly honest, I wasn't anxious to do it. My real interest, as I said, was the long form, and I was supposed to supervise all those two hour movies. I was pretty much strong-armed to do it, and not given too much of a choice. Paramount said, 'Forget the two hour movies, you're doing **Star Trek**.'

> "
>
> At that point, forces were at work which would pull Goodwin away from this choice assignment and bring him over to Roddenberry's team. Meanwhile, Roddenberry himself grew more vibrant with each passing day, as a seven year battle to bring **Star Trek** back seemed at an end.
>
> "

"So I went over to see Gene," he continues, "and initially I got kicked out of his office. His assistant, Susan Sackett, thought I was an agent or something, and she didn't know that I had an appointment to see him. She wouldn't let me in, and I said, 'Fine,' and walked out. I was about a half a mile away at the other side of the studio when Gene Roddenberry came running after me. To make a long story short, he wanted me to go in as one of the two producers. They were going to hire a writing producer and a production producer. It was kind of a strange situation."

Roddenberry found his "writing producer" in Harold Livingston, novelist and veteran television writer.

"I had never met Roddenberry," admits Livingston, "but I think I was working at Paramount at the time. Bob Goodwin and I were both going to work under Gene. If I remember correctly, there were a lot of interviews and bullshit that went on, but Gene and I kind of hit it off. We had similar backgrounds. We had both been in the Air Force during the war and we both worked for civilian airlines after the war, so I think that's one of the reasons that Gene, in the beginning, liked me.

"I had never paid much attention to **Star Trek**," he smiles sheepishly. "I'd always considered it something of a media event. I was totally unwashed. Anyway, the object of the new series was very vague. All they knew was that the studio had some kind of arrangement with what was then going to be a fourth network. I suppose it would take the form of some kind of syndicated program. So thirteen episodes plus a pilot were ordered, and it was then my job to develop these stories, which I set upon doing."

To this end, he began to utilize Jon Povill, Gene Roddenberry's assistant.

"I wanted Jon Povill to be my story editor," he explains, "and Gene wanted him to continue cleaning his garage or something, so we had a big thing about that. I eventually got my way."

"Harold was primarily responsible for getting me the story editor job," concurs Povill. "Gene was reluctant to move me 'that far, that fast,' to use his words. Harold was adamant that I was doing the job of a story editor and, by God, I should be getting paid as one.

"Harold had not been very familiar with the old series at all," he continues, "and kind of relied on me to be the monitor of whether something fit with **Star Trek** or not. Once everything got rolling,

> " Gene and I kind of hit it off. We had similar backgrounds. We had both been in the Air Force during the war. "

and we were in a lot of writer's meetings, I sort of took over as the person who pointed out where there were holes in the stories, and where they did not conform to what **Star Trek** was supposed to be."

Rounding out the early cast of behind-the-scenes characters was Jim Rugg, a veteran from the original series who was to handle the special effects, and production designer Joe Jennings. Matt Jeffries, who had designed the original Enterprise, but was, at the moment, tied up on **Little House on the Prairie**, would serve as technical consultant.

No sooner had the television series been announced, than Gene Roddenberry received a letter from one irate fan who had recently attended a convention and was totally appalled at what he considered to be a "make-a-buck" attitude on the part of the people behind it. Roddenberry took this to heart and sent a memo to Gary Nardino in which he expressed his concern that a reporter might get his hands on something like this. In such a situation, he found it easy to imagine coast-to-coast stories on how **Star Trek** rips off kids. He was fearful that this would happen, unless they took steps to "protect our show and our image." This brief memo proved that everything about this new **Star Trek** was being taken quite seriously.

On July 15, 1977, Gene Roddenberry issued a memo telling the production crew that they needed to come up with a new bible for potential writers. Bob Goodwin, Harold Livingston, Jon Povill and several others began making contributions to this item, which had proved a successful tool during the course of the original series. The "bible" which eventually evolved, stated that the series would chronicle the second five year mission of the Enterprise. While in drydock following its initial mission, the vessel had been completely refurbished.

James T. Kirk, we learn, has refused a promotion to admiral so that he can command the starship on its newest voyage. All of his original crew have been reassigned to him, with the exception of Mr. Spock, who has "returned in high honor to Vulcan to head the Science Academy there." In updating the series and attempting to fill the void created by Spock's absence, three new characters were added and hopes were high that actor Leonard Nimoy would frequently reprise his role of Spock for guest appearances.

In the guide, Roddenberry, who would make similar statements when originally discussing **Star Trek: The Next Generation**

"

On July 15, 1977, Gene Roddenberry issued a memo telling the production crew that they needed to come up with a new bible for potential writers. Bob Goodwin, Harold Livingston, Jon Povill and several others began making contributions.

"

nearly a decade later, wrote, "We will use science fiction to make comments on today, but today is now a dozen years later than the first **Star Trek**. Humanity faces many new questions and puzzles which were not obvious back in the 1960's, all of them suggesting new stories and themes."

Defining the basis of a **Star Trek** story, the guide notes that such stories are about people, and not science or gadgetry; that each should always be told from the point of view of Captain Kirk and the crew, that the regular characters are heroes and should always react as such, and that home base is the Enterprise.

From here, the guide details the intricacies of the Enterprise's weapon and defense abilities, followed by a character breakdown, focusing on the new additions.

Lt. Xon, a full Vulcan, has taken the place of Mr. Spock as ship science officer. This twenty year old, who is "a genius even by Vulcan standards," was destined to prove himself as capable as his predecessor. The primary difference between the two is that Xon has virtually no knowledge of the human equation, and realizes that the only way he will be able to equal Spock is by making an effort to touch his repressed emotions, thus allowing him to more fully relate to the crew. Roddenberry wrote that "we'll get some humor out of Xon trying to simulate laughter, anger, fear and other human feelings." Interesting to note is that the Spock-McCoy feud would have carried over to Xon and the doctor, with the difference being that McCoy believes their "feud is a very private affair ... and McCoy has been known to severely chastise (in private) those crewmen who have been unfair to the Vulcan in comparing his efforts to Spock's."

The second new character mentioned is Commander Will Decker, Enterprise first officer who is something of a young Captain Kirk. The son of Commodore Matt Decker, who met his demise tackling "The Doomsday Machine," he comes quite close to worshipping the captain, and would "literally rather die than fail him." This is in direct contrast to the somewhat antagonistic Kirk-Decker relationship demonstrated in **Star Trek: The Motion Picture**. Essentially Decker is a captain-in-training, and the idea was that the audience would watch his gradual growth during the five year mission. In many instances, he would lead landing parties, thus alleviating the perpetual logistical flaw of the initial **Star Trek** TV series: a ship's captain would never beam into

We will use science fiction to make comments on today, but today is now a dozen years later than the first **Star Trek**. Humanity faces many new questions and puzzles which were not obvious back in the 1960's, all of them suggesting new stories and themes.

49

potential danger as often as Kirk did. It's a format change which would eventually be incorporated into **The Next Generation**, where Riker rather than Captain Picard leads advance teams.

In a sense, this would make the situation more logical and would have given the Decker character an opportunity to develop. In addition, we could have witnessed Kirk's frustration at not always being directly involved with beam-downs.

The final new addition to the crew would have been Lieutenant Ilia, the bald Deltan, whose race is marked by a heightened sexuality that pervades every aspect of their society. Additionally, Ilia, as is common among her people, is abnormally intelligent, second, perhaps, only to Xon, and gifted with some rather unique esper abilities. As noted, "unlike the mind-meld of Vulcans, it simply is the ability to sense images in other minds. Never words or emotions, only images ... shapes, sizes, textures. On her planet, sexual foreplay consists largely of lovers placing images in each other's minds." Like Decker, Ilia made it into the first feature film, and remained, essentially, as the guide depicted her.

These character profiles were followed by a breakdown of the original crew, an explanation of the standing sets, descriptions of equipment and an explanation of terminology. It concluded with some very basic questions, followed by the appropriate answers. For instance:

"Q: What is Earth like in **Star Trek**'s century?

A: For one thing, we'll seldom take a story back there and, therefore, don't expect to get into subjects which would create great problems, technical and otherwise. The U.S.S. on our ship stands for 'United Space Ship'—indicating without troublesome specifics that mankind has found some unity on Earth, perhaps at long last even peace. If you require a statement such as one that Earth cities of the future are splendidly planned with fifty mile parkland strips around them, fine."

The **Star Trek** feature films have provided tantalizing hints of the future, but never delved into it in great detail. Perhaps the new series eventually will, although it isn't likely. Some things, one would assume, are best left to the imagination. Nonetheless, the show's bible was an efficient guide to the dos and don'ts of **Star Trek II**.

"

Q: What is Earth like in **Star Trek**'s century?

A: For one thing, we'll seldom take a story back there and, therefore, don't expect to get into subjects which would create great problems, technical and otherwise. The U.S.S. on our ship stands for 'United Space Ship'—indicating without troublesome specifics that mankind has found some unity on Earth, perhaps at long last even peace. If you require a statement such as one that Earth cities of the future are splendidly planned with fifty mile parkland strips around them, fine.

"

With the guide having been written, Harold Livingston began contacting writers and agents in an effort to get the first thirteen scripts in motion.

"I wanted to make **Star Trek** more universal," explains Livingston matter of factly. "I felt that success not withstanding, the show had a restrictive audience. There was a greater audience for this. I felt that almost all of the stories seemed to be allegorical, and I wanted to make them a little harder and a little more realistic. My broad intention was to create a series that would attract a larger audience by offering more. We would still offer the same elements that **Star Trek** did, i.e. science fiction and hope for the future, and do realistic stories.

"I just thought they had reached a certain barrier with it," he continues. "How much could you do before it becomes totally redundant, and then where do you go? I wanted to bring it down to Earth ... figuratively. They had so many stories which, to manipulate or move the plot, this goofy thing appeared out of nowhere. I'm thinking specifically of some Greek with an echoing voice that came on and saved them. That was done too often. And I simply also wanted scripts that were interesting and made sense and moved from a literary standpoint. I felt that too much of that was neglected or overlooked, because they had their science fiction themes. I wanted to do both, although I don't know if it would have worked. I have a great fear of these cultist series-films, because they're really self defeating in the end. You're going to have a limited audience. That was my feeling, right or wrong."

Requests for stories went out to a variety of people, all of whom had experience either in **Star Trek**, science fiction or writing the genre for television. Everything was coming together smoothly, and on July 28, 1977, Jon Povill made note of a story he had received from the show's NASA technical advisor, Jesco Von Puttkamer. Entitled "The Sleeping God," it dealt with a being named Singa whose brain is so incredibly powerful that he is kept in suspended animation to conserve the resource. This being serves the Federation.

"In the other corner," said Povill, "from another universe, is Nahga, more or less a mutated super computer that has succeeded in the ultimate narcissism. It has studied and destroyed all competing forms of intelligence throughout its entire universe. Now it

> " I have a great fear of these cultist series-films, because they're really self defeating in the end. You're going to have a limited audience. "

has opened a corridor into ours and has sent its first war machines through it. They have thus far been unstoppable; destroying several Federation and Klingon planets."

Naturally the Enterprise finds itself in the middle, and Kirk must use everything at his command, including Singa, to enter the Nahga's realm, and stop this threat to his own universe.

"I think there are useable elements here," Povill pointed out, "but the story as it stands would cost about five million to do."

That fact alone seemed enough to stop conversations pertaining to the story, although it did eventually appear in one of Bantam Books's *Star Trek: The New Voyages*.

The next day, famed science fiction author Norman Spinrad wrote to Harold Livingston regarding a story the two men had discussed, that essentially dealt with the search for ultimate knowledge as well as personality changes in some of our crewmembers [see "To Attain the All" in the Appendix].

On August 4, Gene Roddenberry referred to the story by saying, "We could use any ideas [which] might make this story work. Spinrad is brilliant and he is onto the right thing." Negatively speaking, he noted that the production probably couldn't afford the maze as described in the story. "Also," he explained, "it is largely a two-man story with them interacting with a 'hidden power.' It is hardly action-adventure. The jeopardy is mostly intellectual."

The entire **Star Trek II** company was very excited by Spinrad's full treatment which came later on. Roddenberry in particular was extremely positive, suggesting that perhaps the alien power could sway the Enterprise crew over by offering to give the individual whatever it was they desired most. This, he pointed out, was similar to, but different from, the premise of the original show's first season episode, "The Naked Now." Interestingly enough, the idea of trying to sway the crew by offering them wha they desire most was picked used in the "Hide and Q" episode of the **Next Generation**.

"I don't remember where the idea came from," Spinrad admits, "except that I've always been fascinated with the high-mind concept, which I have dealt with in books. It would have made a great TV piece, because it's all in the acting. They all take on each other's characteristics, which is something really weird and

> " We could use any ideas (which) might make this story work. Spinrad is brilliant and he is onto the right thing. "

strange, that wouldn't be as interesting in a novel. But would be as a film or play, something oral. Something with acting."

In Patrick Duncan's "The Phaethon Derelict," which reached Povill on August 1, 1977, the Enterprise encounters a planetoid that turns out to be a space vehicle from Earth, launched in the 21st Century, and it's populated by the descendents of the original crew. The ship's propulsion units have long since failed, and it was thought lost or destroyed long ago. A landing party from the Enterprise beams over, and they discover a race which has based its religion on Starfleet directives. Kirk wants to help these people, but the Prime Directive is now theoretically in effect in this situation. He cannot alter the natural development of this society. How, then, to save them? That is Kirk's dilemma.

This story holds a variety of similarities to plots we've seen before, most notably to Robert Heinlein's *Orphans of the Sky* and to the **Trek** episode "For the World is Hollow and I Have Touched the Sky." And to David Gerrold's **The Galactic Whirlpool**, based on the series and his tribute to the Heinlein work.

"There is much bullshit in this story," Povill noted of the outline, "but the basic premise of the derelict planetoid/spaceship— children of **Space 1999** as it were—with a retrogressed culture ... seemed intriguing."

This story, like Puttkamer's, was not taken any further, but it did help to fuel Roddenberry's concern that perhaps they weren't receiving the proper stories for the series.

"Apparently the past has a way of repeating itself," he said on August 4th. "During our first three years, a principal problem in most story ideas received was that they usually presented our captain and crew with no particular *jeopardy* or *need*. In other words, it is not sufficient for a story idea merely to have our people running into something interesting while out in space. In fact, it is not even sufficient to have them run into merely something fascinating!

"The above is why the typical story of 'two interesting civilizations' rarely works out," added Roddenberry. "Too often a writer thinks he has brought in enough if there are needs created for other characters in the story. This simply doesn't work. Yes, we want our **Star Trek** story to involve fascinating things we meet out there, but those fascinating things *must* create an important need for one or more of our characters. That need can be for something to happen—or something *not* to happen. That need

> **"**
>
> There is much bullshit in this story but the basic premise of the derelict planetoid/spaceship— children of **Space 1999** as it were—with a retrogressed culture ... seemed intriguing.
>
> **"**

53

should grow steadily more and more important so story moves toward climax. Also, the resolution of that need must grow more and more impossible. Admittedly, all this is fairly elemental and stuff every writer knows. But I think that *all* of us (including yours truly) often tend to forget it when doing science fiction."

One of the writers contacted was Alan Dean Foster, author of numerous genre novels, including the *Star Trek Log* series for Ballantine Books.

"Roddenberry had gotten in touch with me because of the *Log* series," Foster recalls. "He felt that I was comfortable with the **Star Trek** universe, and familiar with the characters. So I submitted three story ideas, one of which was based on a page and a half outline for 'Robot's Return,' an episode of **Genesis II**. He thought that could be developed and wanted to see what I could do with it. So that was one of the three things I took home and developed into story ideas which ran about five or six pages each. One of them, which I would still like to do, involved the Enterprise arriving at a planet which was the 1860's south, only the white folks were the slaves and the black folks were the ruling class. Anyway, Roddenberry told me to develop the story for 'In Thy Image' into a full scale treatment. After it was turned in, it was decided to open the series with a two hour movie for TV, which is fairly standard practice when they can manage it. Of the treatments at hand, mine was the best suited to carry two hours, so I went home and developed the outline further."

"Robot's Return" dealt with a space probe returning to Earth after hundreds of years, and in search of its creator NASA. "In Thy Image" took this basic premise [See the Appendix under "In Thy Image" for full plot information] and placed it in the **Star Trek** universe, enlarging the overall threat along the way as Kirk and company must save the entire planet from this deadly machine.

"At that point," interjects Bob Goodwin, "they had spent about four years trying to get a script for a feature, but they couldn't come up with anything that Michael Eisner liked. We had various options on the two hour premiere [which would be released theatrically in Europe], and I suggested to Gene that since it had never been done in the series before, we should come up with a story in which Earth was threatened. In all the **Star Trek** episodes before, they never came close to Earth. 'In Thy Image' fit that criteria perfectly.

> " They had spent about four years trying to get a script for a feature, but they couldn't come up with anything that Michael Eisner liked. "

"I remember," he adds, "that one day we went into the administration building. In there was Michael Eisner, Jeff Katzenberg, Gary Nardino, me, Gene and a bunch of other people. In the course of that meeting, I got up and pitched this two-hour story. Michael Eisner slammed his hands on the table and said, 'We've spent four years looking for a feature script. This is it. Now let's make the movie.'"

The plan still called for a two hour television film, but no one in that room realized that the groundwork had just been laid down for **Star Trek: The Motion Picture**.

CHAPTER VII

The atmosphere of that meeting, held on August 3, 1977, was a combination of joy and sobriety. On the one hand it was proof that **Star Trek** was very much alive in Paramount's eyes, and on the other it revealed how problematic resurrecting the show actually was.

Meeting with Michael Eisner, Jeff Katzenberg and other key executives, Gene Roddenberry stated at the outset that he expected to have up to ten scripts in development within a two week time period. Michael Eisner felt that their primary concern must be the two-hour opening episode. It would kick off the new series and tap into the "enormous amount of worldwide potential in the first return of **Star Trek**. A February 1st answer print is vital, and the film must be superb."

While Roddenberry agreed with this, his general feeling was that the more stories they got into development, the wider their choice of an opening story would be. "The intention," he said, "is to give the best material to top established writers."

Michael Eisner, without hesitation, pointed out that he had no problems with paying whatever writing cost was necessary to insure the best possible script. He even went so far as to state a willingness to pay up to two hundred thousand dollars for the script. Another concern was the lack of a director, although Gary [**The Black Hole**] Nelson was being talked to, with Bob Collins as a backup.

Eisner continued to emphasize how important it was for them to meet the February 1st date, and for the story to be finalized so preproduction could begin.

"We'd be kidding you if I didn't say we have some problems on the February 1st date, but we're hoping to overcome them," Roddenberry explained.

"Look," Eisner responded, "I'm willing to go with a three million dollar budget, if the script is good enough. I'm not encouraging extravagance, but I am concerned that we meet the target date and the film be visually fabulous. We need a writer who can make the characters come alive, with a terrific director and a terrific story."

Changing the subject for a moment, Gene Roddenberry admitted that he was bothered by the idea of tailoring the opening script to both William Shatner and Leonard Nimoy, as the latter would not

> "
>
> Michael Eisner felt that their primary concern must be the two-hour opening episode. It would kick off the new series and tap into the enormous amount of worldwide potential in the first return of **Star Trek**.
>
> "

be a part of the regular series. "I'd prefer to eliminate Nimoy completely," he said.

Eisner disagreed, stating that it was absolutely necessary for them to have both actors reprising their original roles, even if they must be signed at unreasonable figures.

"I don't agree," countered Roddenberry. "I can almost promise us that the excitement generated by the return of **Star Trek** with most of the original crew, aided by a publicity campaign to hype excitement over the new, different type of Vulcan, would cancel out any disappointment over Nimoy's absence."

The Paramount chieftain would not accept this. The actor, he insisted again, must appear in the film, even if only briefly during the opening scenes. Both Roddenberry and Goodwin agreed, feeling that it would be a preferable way of handling the situation, because it would satisfy audience demand while at the same time allowing them the freedom to work with the new story and characters.

As stated earlier, one reason Nimoy didn't wish to appear on the series was due to a lawsuit he launched against Paramount. The actor felt he should be compensated for the money Paramount was making from his likeness on **Star Trek** merchandise. Gary Nardino explained that a deal had been offered to the actor which would include the opening film, select episodes and a settlement of his lawsuit against them. In response, Eisner said that he would be willing to pay the actor up to $100,000 for three days of work, but the deal with Shatner should be closed first so as to keep his cost down.

"It's understood," he added, "that there's no interest in him for the series, although we may have to make a pay-or-play PTS [Paramount Television Service] commitment as incentive for the two hour film."

Roddenberry again stated that he was concerned about making the February 1st date, and Eisner explained that he was attempting to generate money abroad on the property before it went to television. Approval was given to put thirteen scripts into work for series delivery in March 1978, but no series problems/ deadlines should effect the two hour film.

> "
> Eisner disagreed, stating that it was absolutely necessary for them to have both actors (Shatner and Nimoy) reprising their original roles, even if they must be signed at unreasonable figures.
> "

"There is only one priority at Paramount," Eisner stated emphatically: "**Star Trek**."

CHAPTER VIII

In attempting to bring **Star Trek** back to audiences of the 1970's, the show found itself saddled with a problem. It had to be overcome for the series to work.

"The original series had seventy nine episodes," points out Jon Povill, "and therefore a lot of things had already been done. I think the biggest challenge was coming up with things that weren't repeats of ideas which had already been explored. What we were definitely striving for on the show was doing things that were different, and I think by and large we were successful. That was the biggest challenge, coming up with things that were fresh, and were **Star Trek** as well.

"I think we were helped out tremendously by the new characters. It's something that the features really need at this point. Someone has to start taking over. I think it's absolutely essential. They're all good people and they're just right for their parts, but if you don't start setting something up here, they're going to start ... no offense to anybody ... dying off. The characters of Xon, Decker and Ilia would have helped in this area. We wanted characters that could go in new directions, as well as the old crew.

"I particularly liked Xon," says Povill. "I thought there was something very fresh in having a nice young Vulcan to deal with; somebody who was trying to live up to a previous image. That, to me, was a very nice gimmick for a TV show that was missing Spock. But we *never* wanted Xon to be a Spock retread. We wanted him to be somebody who definitely had his own direction to go in, and he had different failings than Spock. Also, he didn't have Spock's neurosis regarding his human half. As far as Xon was concerned, Spock had a distinct *advantage* in being half-Vulcan and half-human in the context of where he was, what he was doing and where he was working. If he was on Vulcan, it wouldn't have been an advantage, but to be living with humans, it really helped. Xon's youth was also very important and he would have brought a freshness that people would have appreciated.

"Ilia was sort of an embodiment of warmth, sensuality, sensitivity and a nice Yin to Xon's Yang. Decker, of course, was a young Kirk. I think he would have been the least distinct. He would have had to grow, and the performance probably would have done that, bringing something to Decker that the writers would have ultimately latched on to for material. He's the one who

> **"**
> The biggest challenge was coming up with things that weren't repeats of ideas which had already been explored.
> **"**

59

> "
>
> Most of my comments will bear upon control and selective use of that imagination. *Believability* of characters, incidents and scenes is much more critical in picture/sound science fiction than in printed .... Most of our story problem seems to boil down simply to getting to know our alien machine character better.
>
> "

would have had to develop more through the acting and performance than the other two. Xon and Ilia were concept characters. They would have developed too, I'm sure, because characters grow when they're performed much more than they do from just the writing. In the early writing, you don't realize the full potential. You don't know who's going to play the character, how they're going to play it and what the characteristics of their performance are going to be. If you look at 'The Menagerie,' for example, Spock laughs."

On August 9th, Roddenberry responded to Alan Dean Foster's one hour treatment of "In Thy Image."

"The principal problem in your **Star Trek** story outline is certainly not lack of imagination," he pointed out. "Rather, I believe, most of my comments will bear upon control and selective use of that imagination. *Believability* of characters, incidents and scenes is much more critical in picture/sound science fiction than in printed .... Most of our story problem seems to boil down simply to getting to know our alien machine character better. Its abilities, limitations, motivations, needs, and so on. With all that established, it should then be much easier to build a tale which rises steadily in excitement and jeopardies (to the starship *and* to Earth) to a very exciting and satisfying climax."

Ironically, this problem would plague the script even after it had metamorphosized into **Star Trek: The Motion Picture**. It was a thematic trap no one could extricate themselves from.

While Alan Dean Foster took Roddenberry's comments to heart and began to expand his outline, **Star Trek II** was coming to life on the Paramount soundstages. On August 9, Bob Goodwin filed his first production report.

"Work is continuing on stage 9," he explained, "with construction of the Enterprise set. All frames and platforms have been built for the bridge ... By tomorrow we will have a lay-out on the stage floor for the corridor and by the beginning of next week we will start framing and constructing the corridor walls. Joe Jennings has worked out most of the design problems of the engineering room and has started working on drawings which will be ready for you to see by the end of the week ... The plan now for stage 8, which will be used as the planet set is to put in the ground row and the backing, but to leave the dirt out until we see if we need that stage space for any extra sets that might be needed for our first show."

As all this was developing, production designer Joseph Jennings was in the midst of creating the interior of a starship which would be completely unlike the rather primitive looking sets of the original **Star Trek**.

"I had been working at Paramount," explains Jennings, "and the Production Manager of Television called me in and said, 'How would you like the assignment?' We started preparing and that was about it. It was as simple as that."

In attempting to upgrade the ship from the original series, he says that the idea was to make the mechanics of the starship much more sophisticated.

"The bridge of the Enterprise," he adds, "was designed to go into series, so we were designing it to be all things to all people. As a result, all of the devices were practical and they worked off proximity switches. You didn't have to touch the board, but simply had to reach toward it and whatever effect you were tripping would show up. This was not for one specific show. What you're being asked to do is design a set that will function for at least three years of shows, so we were being a great deal more sophisticated than perhaps we would have been were it laid out to begin with as a feature film in which there were a certain given set of actions that had to be performed on that set. Then you only build those things that operate properly.

Work is continuing on stage 9 with construction of the Enterprise set. All frames and platforms have been built for the bridge ... By tomorrow we will have a lay-out on the stage floor for the corridor and by the beginning of next week we will start framing and constructing the corridor walls.

61

> " I wrote an operations manual for the bridge, which was intended to be given to guest directors who would come in and would not be familiar with the set, but in a matter of several days would have to come up with a working knowledge of it. So all of the stations and every switch, button and light flash was all spelt out as to what it did and what it was supposed to be. "

"When you talk about series," Jennings elaborates, "you don't know down the line what you're going to need. As a result, I wrote an operations manual for the bridge, which was intended to be given to guest directors who would come in and would not be familiar with the set, but in a matter of several days would have to come up with a working knowledge of it. So all of the stations and every switch, button and light flash was all spelt out as to what it did and what it was supposed to be. It was an attempt on my part to make the operation of the ship consistent from show to show. As I say, all of that effort and energy when it became a picture was superfluous. To be specific, directors walk in on the bridge of a spaceship and want every damn light winking and blinking, and now you get your spaceship in trouble and the meteor is coming. What do you add to it that's going to look dramatic? Besides, if you look on the instrument panel of any comparable vehicle we know, all of those lights aren't blinking all the time. So I thought perhaps by being very specific in making the thing operable, we could get a little more believability into it from that point of view."

Jennings strived for more logical designs, with small details which would have added a certain sense of realism to the show. For instance, it was his feeling that the seats on the bridge should have protective devices to keep the crew locked in them during a crisis.

"We always had problems with those bridge chairs going clear back to the original series," he laughs, "because quite obviously if the technology was capable of doing what our script said it was capable of doing, it would have been capable of developing a chair in which an operator could be protected, and yet every time they ran into a meteor, they wanted everybody to fall out of their chair. We built all those nice protective restraints so they couldn't fall out of their chairs. What's a director going to do? I mean, they shake their camera like crazy and everybody sits firmly in their seats.

"Who's going to believe that?" he asks wryly.

A second addition to the bridge was a large bubble near the weapons console which would serve, in effect, as a tactical tracking device.

"I can't remember at what point that was taken out," Jennings admits. "Again, this was pointed towards a series in which everyone knows you're going to constantly be approaching objects in space or objects in space are going to approach you, so it was an attempt at the gunnery sight, if you like. It was a big plastic bubble on the bridge, and we eventually felt we could use miniatures in the bubble and see a 3-D representation of the approaching target.

"That's what was ultimately planned for it, but it created some sound problems and some light problems and they decided they didn't want to work with it. The shapes I was working with provided focus problems. The old Enterprise bridge was pretty much flat-planed, even though it was circular, which was an economy measure. When we decided to upgrade it, it was built in an elliptical section because we then had the money to build molds. All of the consoles were molded right into the walls. It was made to appear that they were all molded together. But that elliptical shape had an echo to it like a whispering gallery. You could say something into one end, go to the other end and hear it. While we still had it in the mock-up stage, we got Glen Glen Sound over and they said it would be no problem. This big bubble created another nexus, so they figured they didn't want to spend that much time with it. I, for one, thought looking out that big front window, which Gene would never let us get rid of, seemed terribly limiting. This was one reason why I had brought up the constructive gunsight, because you could add another string to the bow. It was an auxiliary; another way of looking at things. At any rate, it was removed and became something else. We used that bubble somewhere. Everything was recycled."

Gene Roddenberry pointed out to Jennings that he wanted him and his people to visualize materials all those years in the future which would virtually support no cross section mass at all, this despite the fact it had to be built out of materials that existed today.

"At the same time," Jennings adds, "you still had to make the set workable. People had to live and work there. That was the driving aim for everybody, and justifiably so. That's what we were trying to do. I'm just illustrating the problems that were and were not, which were solved for better or for worse, but were always ongoing and always in the forefront. Another very good idea, and one that goes clear back to the original, was the axiom that the technology was not to be observed. By that I mean a tricorder was like a screwdriver in that you don't say, 'Hey, look at me, I'm moving a screwdriver.' You just pick up the screwdriver and take the screw out. All the technology was to be state-of-the-art

> " It was a big plastic bubble on the bridge, and we eventually felt we could use miniatures in the bubble and see a 3-D representation of the approaching target. That's what was ultimately planned for it, but it created some sound problems and some light problems and they decided they didn't want to work with it. "

63

and people would use it simply as tools. Both the actors' and directors' attitudes were to do that. I always thought that worked very well. The movie, on the other hand, destroyed that because it said, 'Hey look, how do you figure we did this?'

"The great proper use of that sort of thing was **Star Wars**. George Lucas was smart enough to get off of the special effects and you said, 'Jesus, did I see what I think I saw?' That's where you want to be. My kids went back three times to see how they did it, and they still couldn't figure it out. It was there just long enough to establish the idea and get off it before they figure out what's going on. Then you go away with your imagination working on overtime, and I guarantee you that you'll think you saw a great deal more than you actually did. This is where **Star Trek** fell down. It was almost like for once the little boy had all the candy he could possibly eat, and what did he do? He ate himself sick. In other words, artistically they were far better off as a series than a film. It's driven to economy, as is all good art."

Another innovation was the idea of having mini-transporters located throughout the Enterprise so that small objects which were needed in different areas could instantly be beamed over. This, again, was an attempt to set up a certain number of givens for what was still intended to be a weekly series.

"As I said earlier, the ship was designed to be all things to all people, because once you've established the thing, it's established. It's like I spent eight years doing **Gunsmoke**, and once we had a director who decided that because of a piece of business, he wanted the stove in Matt's office downstage so that somebody could come down towards the camera and get the coffee pot. We moved it, and we received all kinds of mail telling us that that's not where the stove belongs.

"This is part of series television," Jennings concludes on the subject. "Your audience has a running familiarity with the surroundings, so as a result you can use pre-established areas. When Spock heads up to the science station, you know where he's going. You don't have to stop and somehow explain it to the audience."

In the meantime, on August 16th Harold Livingston filed a "writers status report," noting that those assigned included Arthur Heinemann, Alan Dean Foster, James Menzies, Margaret Armen, John Meredyth Lucas, Worley Thorne, Shimon Wincelberg and

> "
> This is where **Star Trek** fell down. It was almost like for once the little boy had all the candy he could possibly eat, and what did he do? He ate himself sick.
> "

Theodore Sturgeon. Of them, only Sturgeon would not ultimately deliver a story.

In addition, Livingston met with a total of seventeen other writers, of which only Bill Lansford had a story which fit **Star Trek** requirements. Entitled "Devil's Due," the producer noted that he and Roddenberry had met with the author "concerning a story with Faustian overtones, a Devil and Daniel Webster conflict and we expect to assign Lansford after a final meeting."

While these meetings did not bear much fruit, Livingston was still quite pleased at the way things were progressing. "We find that these initial meetings are beneficial to writers," he said, "because despite the writer's guide and the two scripts we usually give as representative **Star Trek** scripts, it is always helpful when the writers discuss face to face and we explain our problems, requirements, standards and specifications. With almost no exception, writers have recontacted us and/or have reacted enthusiastically."

The memo concluded with Livingston pointing out that they had not yet evaluated Alan Dean Foster's two-hour episode, but that it would be done shortly so that they could determine who would write the actual script, as the producer had elected *against* Foster doing so.

"Alan brought me two screenplays, which I wasn't very impressed with," he recalls, "and I didn't want him to write the script. This is obviously a subjective opinion, but that's what they were paying me for. It was my judgement that they should get someone else."

Nearly two weeks later, he submitted a list of twenty more writers he had met with. Only a handful were encouraged to develop their stories further for a second meeting. Two names on the list were **Star Trek** veterans: David Gerrold and Carey Wilbur.

"We have also received a large number of submissions from various writers," said Livingston, "either in one or two page outlines, and in some cases full scripts. We have investigated most of these, but none have really met **Star Trek** standards. They keep coming in and the response from writers is totally overwhelming."

He added that the search had begun for a writer to flesh "In Thy Image" out to script form. His first choice, Steven Bochco (**Hill Street Blues, L.A. Law**) was unavailable and would be for sev-

> "
> We have also received a large number of submissions from various writers either in one or two page outlines, and in some cases full scripts. We have investigated most of these, but none have really met **Star Trek** standards.
> "

eral months. Two other names being considered were British author David Ambrose (who would ultimately pen the "Deadlock" script for the proposed series) and science fiction veteran William Norton. An attempt to interest Michael Cimino was unfruitful, which is probably just as well. Imagine "Heaven's Trek."

"The problem with many name writers," Livingston opined, "is that we do not want to involve ourselves in a situation where we will sign a writer who will be tempted to 'write down' to the story. We must have someone who is actively into science fiction, namely **Star Trek**, and will be so enthusiastic he will give us the very best he has.

After four weeks of developing stories, talking to writers, word has come back to us now and it is very interesting to note that **Star Trek** is considered the 'hardest sell in town.'

"After four weeks of developing stories," he closed, "talking to writers, word has come back to us now and it is very interesting to note that **Star Trek** is considered the 'hardest sell in town.' It is also considered perhaps the most prestigious credit a writer can receive. This, needless to say, we consider very encouraging. The result has been that we are very selective in our story material, and we feel that the stories we now have in work are the best possible stories we could find. Our status now is that we have eleven hours assigned. This includes two two-hour versions. This would leave us with two one-hour openings. We have requested the purchase of an additional five back-up hours, and are anxiously awaiting approval on this request."

Bob Collins, in the meantime, had been signed to direct the opening episode, and began to help in the screentesting process to determine who would be most suited to portray the pair of alien characters, Xon and Ilia. He elected to begin with the Vulcan, and tested hundreds of actors in pointed ears before he spotted the one he felt most comfortable with to take over the science station from Mr. Spock.

"I found an actor named David Gautreaux to play Xon," Collins recalls. "He was a nice young man and a terrific actor, and all of that would have worked, although there was some concern over how people would react to the fact that there was no Spock."

That question crossed quite a few minds.

Although the general public may not be aware of it, actor David Gautreaux was a part of the **Star Trek II** company for over a year. In fact, plans still called for him to play the role even when the TV series metamorphosized into the first feature film. But then Leonard Nimoy was signed on as Spock, and Xon was dropped at Gautreaux's request.

"I was doing a play at the time," Gautreaux recalls, "trying not to think that I was going to be playing an alien for the rest of my life. Then I spoke to Gene Roddenberry and said, 'What's the story? Did you see that Leonard Nimoy is coming back to play his character? What's going to happen to Xon?' He said, 'Oh, Xon is very much a part of the family and you're very much a part of our family.' I responded, 'Gene, don't allow a character of this magnitude to simply carry Mr. Spock's suitcases on board the ship and then say, 'I'll be in my quarters if anybody needs me.' Give him what I've put into him and what you've put into him. If he's not going to be more a part of it and more noble than that, let's eliminate him.' They continued with the idea of Xon for quite a while."

Gautreaux's involvement began when he screentested for the role with hundreds of others and was the one chosen for the part. This occurred several months before preproduction on **Star Trek II** had begun, thus scripts for the series had been written and preparations made for the two-hour premiere movie.

"I remember walking on the soundstage and they had, of course, rebuilt the Enterprise," he explains, "and I couldn't get over how everything was 3/4 inch plywood. They intended this baby to fly for about seven years, which is different from a movie set which is designed for the moment.

"At one point when I arrived at the studio, they announced that they were not making the pilot, they were actually making a feature film. The idea of the series was put on hold," the actor elaborates. "Why I know all this is that we had to go through a lot of renegotiation of contracts with the actors on pay or play. If they hire you to do something and they don't do it, they still have to pay you. So we all had to be paid for the pilot film which was never shot, and rehired to do the feature film. I had been placed on some kind of a five or six year television series contract, so when I re-signed, I had to negotiate another television contract.

> **"**
>
> I remember walking on the soundstage and they had, of course, rebuilt the Enterprise. I couldn't get over how everything was 3/4 inch plywood. They intended this baby to fly for about seven years.
>
> **"**

67

Their plans were to do the feature and then go ahead with the series itself."

Upon being announced as **Star Trek**'s newest Vulcan, Gautreaux felt that there were two things that had to be done. The first was for Paramount to down-play his signing aboard, with a bare minimum of publicity. The second was that he purchase a television and learn what the phenomenon was all about. The actor explains his views on both points.

"I remember when I was first cast as Xon," Gautreaux reflects. "A fair amount of the fans reacted very strangely. Somebody recently told me that actors in soap operas place themselves in serious jeopardy if they antagonize the favorite character of the show. They, the actor on the street, can be the object of the fans' wrath. That does happen in this business. When **Star Trek II** was announced and I was essentially the replacement for Spock, I received some really strange letters from people saying, 'Don't drink the water,' or somebody was going to drop LSD in my Coca-Cola. It was like poison pen letters, because Spock was God to these people.

"I personally was never a fan," explains Gautreaux. "I never watched the show. I bought a television two weeks after I was actually signed for the role, because I was given an advance large enough to actually do something like that. I was a hard-working, but not-making-money kind of actor. I just thought I had better start watching the show and catching up with this incredible history. Much of the time I would watch the show and say, 'I don't get it,' not thinking of what it would have looked like if I had seen it in '67 or '68, and compared to it television of the time. It was so revolutionary, but to be looking at it in 1978 or 1979, I didn't think that much of it, although it did carry a large philosophical leap of faith that was wonderful for television."

Studying episodes very carefully, Gautreaux got a firm grasp of just what makes a proper Vulcan and began intensive preparations for the role of Xon, attempting to make the character the quintessential representation of that particular race. One of his greatest motivations was the initial description of the character in the screenplay of "In Thy Image," where the Vulcan, smelling rather strongly, has just beamed aboard from a meditative monastery in the Gobi Desert.

"I actually went off on a meditative trek and fasted for ten days," Gautreaux says. "I allowed my hair to grow long, I started re-

> 66
>
> When I was first cast as Xon, a fair amount of the fans reacted very strangely. I received some really strange letters from people saying, 'Don't drink the water,' or somebody was going to drop LSD in my Coca-Cola. It was like poison pen letters, because Spock was God to these people.
>
> 99

searching to be a Vulcan with no emotion. For an actor, that's death. I was looking at it from an actor's point of view, which is how do you appear as having no emotion without looking like a piece of wood? That was my acting objective, and I went to several acting coaches. Jeff Corey is the one who gave me the key of how I could actively play the pure pursuit of logic as being my primary action. Then I felt I needed a physical equivalent, and I followed the teachings of Bruce Lee, who taught about dealing with emotions and a freedom from emotions that allowed you to live in a non-violent world. That's really what he was all about, despite the impression his films gave.

"His methods, his trainings and his students existed in a nonviolent life. The way to do that was to not let anything 'stick.' If somebody hits you, it doesn't stick; it just flies through you. So with a Vulcan dealing with 'lame brain' human beings ... if they said something particularly stupid, or, in the case of Doctor McCoy, something particularly antagonistic, because of the training I had gone through, it would not have the stick effect. It would not attach itself. The idea is that a Vulcan is pursuing something much larger than what is around him at that moment.

"In all honesty, I was looking forward to playing Xon. His actions were tremendous. His strength without size, and the aspect of playing a full Vulcan. When I say that, I mean somebody who had a larger presence than, say, Spock's father, who was a full Vulcan. By presence I mean a more involved presence on the show and in the running of the ship. It was a very exciting premise to be playing. To me, it was a potentially good gig that didn't work out."

As Gautreaux details, despite rehearsals and costume fittings, the **Star Trek II** project, which became a motion picture, was plagued by a series of "never ending" delays. Initial plans called for production to begin in January of 1978, then April and then June. By that date, Robert Wise had been signed to the project as director [which will be discussed in greater depth later in this volume], a fact which, according to the actor, coincided with Gene Roddenberry's withdrawing from the project ... to a certain degree.

"This is supposition on my part, but I don't think Gene liked the direction that Paramount was taking the feature," he opines, "and I don't think he was happy with the choice of director. Robert Wise is a very powerful man in Hollywood. He's a five time Academy Award-winning director. He's a man of great esteem

> 66
>
> I was looking at it from an actor's point of view, which is how do you appear as having no emotion without looking like a piece of wood?
>
> 99

69

and, if I was him, when I arrived on a set, I would instantly remove anything or anybody who had a different point of view. When I say removed, it's like 'This is a Robert Wise film, yes or no, before we start.' When you're that powerful a director, you can walk on the set and say, 'There is no producer, there is no more executive producer. The writer has done his work. Everyone else go home, this is my picture.' And that's the way it is in Hollywood. Wise had certainly risen to that level, and I'm sure if there were interferences it was the usual power struggle that goes on between two powerful men: someone who has developed a concept and the other person who is hired to shoot it. That's always a struggle. I think Paramount thought they needed a wise and elderly hand to wrestle this project and they ended up wrestling it right to the ground. In my eyes, it never took off. It made tons of money, which is wonderful and surprising compared to the energy of the other films."

According to Gautreaux, and there is not a trace of bitterness in his voice, Wise was instrumental in getting Leonard Nimoy to return as Spock. Reportedly the director wanted to know what ingredient was missing from the mix, and when informed, demanded that the situation be rectified. At the time, Nimoy was still involved in the aforementioned lawsuit with Paramount, but the situation was quickly "handled."

"When Leonard saw the carrot being dangled out in front of him, and this is what he admitted to me himself," says Gautreaux, "when they had recast the role, he felt much more aggressive about settling the lawsuit and getting back into it himself.

"[Several years ago] Leonard called and asked me if I would come down to Paramount. I thought it was because of **Star Trek III**. He had a lot of roles to cast, and he wanted to meet with me. We had a nice long conversation, which is on videotape, because he videotaped all of his conversations. It helped him to remember actors. We chit-chatted for a good period of time, and then he came in with what I call the slider, which was, 'How did you feel ... how did it affect you ... essentially, what did it do to your life when I came back and played Mr. Spock, thus removing your character?' I looked at him and was wondering if he was trying to purge himself of something he's felt all this time. I asked him what he meant by that, and he said, 'Well, you were a young man and this was a very big moment in your life. Did I remove that moment?' I looked at him with a thousand thoughts running through my head. My response was, 'Look, I was young, but I

> "
> Then he came in with what I call the slider, which was, 'How did you feel ... how did it affect you ... essentially, what did it do to your life when I came back and played Mr. Spock, thus removing your character?
> "

70

wasn't brand new. I'd been in this business, primarily in the theatre, for a good long time. For me, Xon and **Star Trek** was like a play that opened and closed on opening night, which happens all the time in theatre. I had, and continue to have, another life outside of whatever Xon was or was not to be.' He said, 'That's very good. I was hoping you'd say something like that.' I had no idea that he had put that much investment and thought into the belief that he had upset my life."

This conversation was the whole gist of the meeting between the two men.

Gautreaux, who, as stated earlier, requested that his character be eliminated rather than diminished, eventually wound up playing Commander Branch of the Epsilon 9 space station in two scenes of **Star Trek: The Motion Picture**. Apart from that, he left the show behind, but has managed to retain the most positive aspects of Xon and his preparation for the role.

"I have found ways to put that training to use," Gautreaux says. "I was an avid bowler at the time and a pretty consistent 160 or 170 kind of bowler. Using the principles of an actor working to become a Vulcan increased my bowling to a consistent 220. The primary goal of a Vulcan is to always be removing his energy away from himself and onto the task, the pursuit of logic or the need of the other person who needs what you have to give them. So you're constantly removing the energy from yourself, thus freeing yourself from obstacles. This is what I learned from fasting.

"When we remove three meals a day plus snacking, get past the third or fourth day, which is the real hump stage, the next ten days are gravy. You can go on forever as long as you have some water and some freshly squeezed juices for necessary proteins now and again. But you are so clear. You ask for something, you know exactly what you're asking for. What you find is that human beings are not very good at dealing with straightforward requests. They always want to know about the grey area and the pink area ... they don't want to just give you the black and white. That's what makes life very silly and full of jokes and shenanigans and why things don't get done as well. Vulcans are like Zen and the art of archery. There's no such thing as a target. There's no such thing as an arrow. There's no such thing as a bow. Everything is one motion, and there's no such thing as hitting the target or not hitting the target, because the bow, the arrow and the target are all one.

'For me, Xon and **Star Trek** was like a play that opened and closed on opening night, which happens all the time in theatre. I had, and continue to have, another life outside of whatever Xon was or was not to be.' He said, 'That's very good. I was hoping you'd say something like that.' I had no idea that he had put that much investment and thought into the belief that he had upset my life.

"So in bowling, you remove at least fifty percent of the effort, which is to do things correctly, and concentrate on the game itself. That kind of concentration can be done on anything you do. I use it all the time."

David Gautreaux pauses for a moment, as though trying to make sure he's expressed the enduring influence of the Xon character throughout his professional and personal life.

"I have never personally felt badly, upset or any of those things for not playing Xon," he concludes sincerely. "I've always felt that it was too bad the public didn't get the chance to see this character, given the preparation I had given to it. But for how it enhanced my own life, they paid me a hundredfold."

"Xon took me from a state of physical to a state of metaphysical, which is something that I've never lost."

On August 29, Harold Livingston presented a new writers status report, and noted that they had met with some twenty-odd writers.

"We have also received a large number of submissions from various writers, either in one or two page outlines, and in some cases full scripts," he said. "We have investigated most of these. None have really met **Star Trek** standards. They keep coming in and the response from writers is totally overwhelming. I have recently received a submission from Thomas Ardies, who has published a best selling novel, is a well known novelist and short story writer, and also extremely desirous of doing a **Star Trek**.

"Richard Bach," the producer continued, "the author of *Jonathan Livingston Seagull*, and the current best-selling novel *Illusions*, is a **Star Trek** fan. He has submitted two stories, both of which were so eminently desirable, we purchased them. One story is a tale of a society whose people are, for the most part, repressed and annually release these emotions by viewing their starships in combat with other starships. It is a very entertaining and provocative story, and Bach had submitted a five page outline. Almost simultaneously, Art Lewis, a very accomplished writer, came in with a similar idea. It was decided to graft both of these stories and assign Lewis to develop the story and teleplay. At the same time, Bach's second story is, what we consider a truly representative **Star Trek** vehicle, about a kind of dream world where our crew members become actively and dangerously involved in the dreams of a lady who had been in suspended animation for 200 years, kept alive throughout that time with periodic dreams. Bach is now writing the outline and actually has requested we allow him to do the script first, and if we do not like the script we can drop the project. I encouraged him to write the traditional outline and we would proceed from that point.

"Alan Dean Foster delivered the final draft of the two-hour movie. We met with him extensively, discussed the story, made numerous revisions and I am now in the process of rewriting the first act which we all, in concert, consider too slow. We should have the story ready to show a screenwriter some time this week."

Two days later, Livingston began to express his opinions and ideas concerning the outline of "In Thy Image." We will take a brief interlude here from our tale of the Lost Years to survey these

> " Alan Dean Foster delivered the final draft of the two-hour movie. We met with him extensively, discussed the story, made numerous revisions and I am now in the process of rewriting the first act which we all, in concert, consider too slow. We should have the story ready to show a screenwriter some time this week. "

73

notes. They serve as a historically significant sample of the thought that went into the story which ultimately became the basis for **Star Trek: The Motion Picture**.

"Briefly," he began, "what we discussed in the opening was that it would start out with the Klingon situation (or in fact without it—I can't see what it does for us). Then, we would have an exterior of Starfleet headquarters, gleaming glass and aluminum buildings, manicured lawns, a beautiful sight. This would establish our locale. We then go inside the building and we see Scott; walking up the aisle, approaches a door which is Fleet Captain Kirk's, Chief of Operations. Scott enters. Kirk is in conference, but the Yeoman informs Kirk of his visitor and we find that Kirk is in conference with Commander Will Decker.

"Commander Decker's father, remember, is the famous Matt Decker of 'The Doomsday Machine,' so we will have established that prior relationship. Kirk is just congratulating and/or informing Decker of his new command, which is a Fleet Cruiser. It is Decker's first command. He is the youngest commander in the Fleet, much as Kirk in his time was also. Scott is now in the office and we have a brief introduction and so forth, then Decker leaves to take over his new ship. Kirk has been summoned by the Admiral to an urgent conference. Scott walks with him to the Admiral's office and we have a moment where they can discuss old times or whatever.

"I remind you here that on the Enterprise at present (the Enterprise being in drydock, being refitted and so forth) are Scott, Uhura, Chekov and Sulu, all having been promoted, all in semi-command positions now and they are on the Enterprise helping to design new equipment, to acquaint new crew members with this equipment and, in general, perhaps functioning as Senior Officers would in such situations." [This is similar to an element which was eventually used at the beginning of **Star Trek II: The Wrath of Khan**].

"In the Admiral's office," Livingston continued, "Kirk is apprised of the urgency (the object hurtling toward the Earth which has wiped out the Klingon cruisers). Kirk, as Operations Chief, is asked for the list of available starship captains. He mentions the names of those people he feels qualified to take the Enterprise out on this most critical mission, and is told that of all the captains qualified for this particular mission it should be he, himself. Now Kirk is somewhat uncertain of this, having been in drydock himself for the last several years perhaps, but realizes the urgen-

> "
>
> Kirk, as Operations Chief, is asked for the list of available starship captains. He mentions the names of those people he feels qualified to take the Enterprise out on this most critical mission, and is told that of all the captains qualified for this particular mission it should be he, himself. Now Kirk is somewhat uncertain of this, having been in drydock himself for the last several years.
>
> "

cy and is briefly prevailed upon to take command of the Enterprise. He would like his old crew and is assured of having them, but he needs a first officer and he knows just the man: Decker. He goes to Decker, tells him he would like him to serve on the Enterprise. This of course means to Decker sacrificing his new command. Decker is rather ambivalent, but is convinced by Kirk to accompany him. In this way we move fast, we feel the urgency of the situation and within our next shot is that lovely shot of Kirk and Decker approaching the Enterprise on the shuttle and we get that **2,001** feeling. Then we are on board and off we go.

"I forgot to mention McCoy. I think we probably need a scene with Kirk and McCoy, with McCoy probably being a vet as indicated here and Kirk going to him, asking him to serve. McCoy refusing. And just as simple as this, Kirk realizes McCoy is serious and turns to leave. Suddenly McCoy says, 'Wait.' So that when Kirk is on the Enterprise a few hours later, McCoy is already there. And in that way I think we can eliminate much of the awkwardness that the reunion would hold. It seems it would just slow up the action.

"Now of course," Livingston reminded, "Once under way, the business of Decker acting 'without enthusiasm.' This is not Decker's attitude at all, nor is it any of the other officers. I think they might be a little grudging about this new mission, but they're certainly not going to bitch about it. As a matter of fact, I think they might be rather pleased to serve under Kirk again. By this I don't mean to suggest we have a rah-rah, gung-ho attitude, but the behavior indicated in the outline is wrong, I think. Also, when Xon appears, there may be some humorous aspects in the idea of the bumbling recruit, but I think this ought to be underplayed because Xon is really, no matter what his age, a cool cat. And what our people might react to, actually, is Xon's natural coldness; natural Vulcan coldness. That would perhaps offend some people and then they would remember Spock, who also had that coldness, but he was Spock and this is Xon and we can play that.

"And that opens us up for a scene: Kirk taking Xon aside and explaining that he is working with humans now and he must be a little friendlier, if he can. I don't think we need the scene with Kirk calling Starfleet about his science officer. His science officer is on board and Kirk is going to accept it for better or for worse. I think these attitudes should prevail throughout until, of course, Xon proves himself later on. To make Xon the continual

> In this way we move fast, we feel the urgency of the situation and within our next shot is that lovely shot of Kirk and Decker approaching the Enterprise on the shuttle and we get that **2,001** feeling.

75

butt of jokes, or goad, is wrong. After all, we're on a crucial mission and we're all professionals and I think we should behave as such. Again, especially under the terrific stress and meaning and significance of this particular mission.

"The urgency of the situation is certainly obvious by the very nature," Livingston insisted, "And I think that while the blueprint of the story follows this, I think the writer can easily cull out the superfluous moves and the padding in the outline. It must be leaned out considerably, but that again I think is obvious and I think will be tended to by the writer."

Livingston then proceeded to point out several very specific flaws in the original story. "I've always been bothered by the action, such as on page 13, where the formula for Pi is received by the alien. I think we should set it up so that the attack stops, but we don't know yet exactly what it was that stopped it. We have tried to communicate with it in several different languages. We later find out it was Pi and this is what leads us to, of course, the revelation that we are dealing with a machine.

"On page 14, we have to be very specific that we have foiled the plan to steal information about our defenses.

"On page 19, Act Five—Kirk going for a brief rest in his cabin. This, again, has always bothered me, because I just don't think Kirk at this time, under these circumstances, is going to take a rest in his cabin. I think this has to be adjusted.

"On page 23, the business with Kirk pretending to be a computer, I really can't believe. I think that in some manner we have to communicate with the alien via our own computer, so that it wouldn't be Kirk's voice simulating a computer voice, it would be in some other form, perhaps flashed on a screen or whatever.

"On page 28, I think this is the biggest flaw in the story. McCoy won't act against Kirk's orders and I say, 'why not, what has he got to lose?' Earth is going to be destroyed anyway, so he certainly would try whatever he could to prevent that, so McCoy's rationale in this instance must be that if the information is released to the alien, it contains (the information) all that which might prove very vulnerable to the other planets of the Federation, thus they, the other planets, would therefore conceivably become victims of the alien because of the information we have provided, so this is why McCoy refuses to allow Xon to release the records. Earth might be destroyed, but at least they've saved the other planets. So that now at least you have a valid motive for

> "
>
> On page 14, we have to be very specific that we have foiled the plan to steal information about our defenses.
>
> "

McCoy's behavior, which opens the way for Decker to make that momentous decision to allow the release of their records and consequently prove himself an officer with the ability to make such a command decision.

"The above is really only a general review of the 'big' holes in the story," Livingston concluded. "I haven't at all addressed myself to all the small details, because I think we should do that in a meeting with the writer and get it over all at once.

"Again, I think the general outline and structure of the story is workable, but I certainly agree on all the many little points that must be fixed to make the story work properly. But I think again, in general, we have a very, very workable story and assuming the writer shares our enthusiasm."

I do believe we'll come out with a very good script.

By the time we return to our tale of the Lost Years in early September, several treatments had arrived at the **Star Trek II** offices, including James Menzies' "The Prisoner," Shimon Wincelberg's "Lord Bobby," William Lansford's "Devil's Due" and the Margaret Armen/Alf Harris collaboration, "The Savage Syndrome."

"The Prisoner" deals with the Enterprise being captured by an alien being who first appears in the form of Albert Einstein to appeal to the crew, but whose real plan is to actually take over the minds of all of humanity. The being cites man's savage nature as his rationale for doing so, and points to several examples of this savagery. Kirk's response is that the items being discussed are ancient history, but the alien believes that man as a species will never change.

"I don't clearly recall the genesis of 'The Prisoner,'" says Harold Livingston, "but I think it happened in our first flush when we were anxious to put projects into work. Overanxious. The basic problem is that nothing happens—none of the characters are very interesting. The idea of the being manifesting itself in the form of Albert Einstein is interesting, but it doesn't pay off. Analyzing the story—and the premise—you begin to see that it *can't* pay off: there simply is not enough substance."

"The Prisoner" would probably not have made a very effective episode. The plot is a mixture of such original series episodes as "The Squire of Gothos," "Return to Tomorrow" and "The Savage Curtain." A variation of the theme would eventually be utilized in the "Encounter at Farpoint" episode of **The Next Generation**, with Q condemning man for his savage tendencies.

"Lord Bobby," which would eventually be retitled "Lord Bobby's Obsession," was a better attempt to present an alien being, again something like Trelene in "Squire of Gothos," as well as the Romulans.

"The Savage Syndrome" had Decker, McCoy and Ilia investigate a derelict vessel in orbit around a lifeless planet. On board, they find that the crew had been driven mad and killed each other in particularly brutal and savage ways. In the meantime, a space mine detonates in the vicinity of the Enterprise, unleashing energy that effects the crew's neural impulses. Instantly, they, including Kirk, are transformed into savages, and it's up to the trio to set things straight again.

> I don't clearly recall the genesis of 'The Prisoner,' but I think it happened in our first flush when we were anxious to put projects into work. Overanxious.

From a production standpoint, this episode would have been quite important for the simple reason that it was primarily a ship-board story, and therefore more cost effective than the average episode. This had been a problem that occurred during the run of the original series, and has been a constant one on **The Next Generation**.

On September 2, 1977, producer Bob Goodwin wrote, "...in order to do an effective job on our stories that take place in settings other than the Enterprise, and still remain within our financial and production limitations, it is absolutely vital that we have an equal number of ship-board stories ... If we don't have some good Enterprise stories in our back pockets, we could find ourselves with very serious production problems comes December."

The memo specifically cited "The Savage Syndrome" as a perfect example of such a ship bound story. For instance, the first draft of the outline had Decker, McCoy and Ilia actually land the shuttlecraft on the surface of a planet, where they studied the ancient ruins as well as "several other things they encounter." Goodwin made the suggestion that the shuttle be investigating an object in space; this way it "would confine our story, for the most part, to the Enterprise." The second draft of the outline made this adjustment.

Harold Livingston came up with the idea of using 23rd Century technology to fight back against the savages.

"Wouldn't it be more exciting and interesting if either Decker or McCoy—or both—used their brains to outwit [them]?" he asked. "For example, they might use the viewing screens and other instruments to completely enthrall the savages, perhaps on a level of the old 'B' movies, where the white explorer, knowing the moon was due to eclipse, filled the natives with awe and dread when he promised to make the sky dark and (as the eclipse occurred) did!" Livingston was right, and the scene would have played just as effectively as it did when Sam Clemens had his Connecticut Yankee pull the same stunt in King Arthur's court. In fact, a later draft had a scene in the rec room, where McCoy threatens to bring the wrath of the gods upon the primitives. On cue, Decker activates the proper controls and "the walls become a crashing ocean, the air filled with the thunder of the waves and wind. An instant later the ocean becomes a World War II battlefield—shells bursting, cannon fire, and the deafening shrieks of the wounded." From there, the image becomes a raging fire, earthquakes and so on.

In order to do an effective job on our stories that take place in settings other than the Enterprise, and still remain within our financial and production limitations, it is absolutely vital that we have an equal number of ship-board stories ... If we don't have some good Enterprise stories in our back pockets, we could find ourselves with very serious production problems.

These illusionary walls were probably inspired by Ray Bradbury's *The Illustrated Man*, and would eventually make it to **The Next Generation** in the form of the Enterprise's holodeck.

Writer Margaret Armen explains the genesis of the episode from her point of view: "Alf and I started with the *what if?* motif. There's an old saying, 'Scratch the man and the savage bleeds.' So, what if these people from this futuristic, very scientific civilization have something happen to them which strips them down to the basic emotions and drives of the cave? That was the line of thought we pursued."

"Devil's Due" essentially put Captain Kirk in the form of a defense attorney, vieing for the freedom of a planet in a struggle against what appears to be the devil. Jon Povill felt that this story worked very well and that it had "all the elements necessary for a very exciting, involving episode."

While things were shaping up nicely with the various stories coming in, the opening two-hour episode was proving to be something of a problem.

"William Norton was engaged to write it," said Livingston, "but on September 5th he contacted me to say that after considerable agonizing he had reached a conclusion that he could not write a proper **Star Trek** script. Although this set us back considerably in time, I think that in the end his honesty and candor and professionalism will prove beneficial. I personally feel this supports my theory that most writers find it extremely difficult writing a **Star Trek** script unless they have been completely immersed in it for some time. **Star Trek** stories require special treatment, special handling; the writers really should be well acquainted with the nuance, characterization and various other colorations that make **Star Trek** stories the unique things that they are.

"This situation," he continued, "needless to say, leaves us in a serious state, bordering on crisis. If we are to meet the November 1st production date it is essential we receive a script no later than October 1st. We have examined and re-examined and re-examined again the names of writers considered qualified to write this initial episode."

None seemed suited for the job, so as a solution to the problem, Livingston set to work on the script himself over the next few weeks. "It is a step not taken likely," he added, "but as something we feel we cannot avoid and leaves us no choice other than to proceed in this manner."

> What if these people from this futuristic, very scientific civilization have something happen to them which strips them down to the basic emotions and drives of the cave?

81

> All of the stories that have come in present no great problems, but all seem to need some work to get them into second draft and subsequently into script. The 'emergency' situation we are faced with slows us up somewhat now in that I am involved writing the script and am unable to devote full time to story development.

As he dove into the first draft script of "In Thy Image," he managed to issue yet another writer's status report in which he explained that there were only three remaining stories to be filled, and that they were being very selective as to which ones they went with.

"All of the stories," he said, "that have come in present no great problems, but all seem to need some work to get them into second draft and subsequently into script. The 'emergency' situation we are faced with slows us up somewhat now in that I am involved writing the script and am unable to devote full time to story development. However, Jon Povill has been very helpful in this area and is keeping things balanced until I can get back to devoting my full attention to this."

Regarding the development of "In Thy Image," he felt that the script was turning out "extremely promising," and that the visuals would be spectacular and easily achieve the "big screen" effect that each of them had been looking for.

"The hour episode situation," Livingston concluded, "is, as I have stated above, somewhat uncertain because of this 'emergency.' Although we would prefer some time on the back, I think with some diligent efforts on all our parts, we'll be able to overcome the time problem and when the two hour-episode is in production, we fully anticipate having enough hour scripts to go forward immediately.

"In essence, then, everything is under control."

Not exactly.

B y the time Harold Livingston had taken to writing "In Thy Image," the working relationship between Livingston and Gene Roddenberry had begun to disintegrate ... badly.

"I don't remember when I began to pierce the Roddenberry myth," Livingston says, "but he and I suddenly started to have creative differences. I resented his interference and he, apparently, wanted someone to carry his lunch around, and that wasn't me. We became socially friendly for a while, but in any case we started to have various difficulties. Out here they're called 'creative differences.' I just didn't think he was a good writer, and I didn't like the way he was doing some of the material. He, for his part I'm sure, considered me a total interloper. After all, who the hell was I to come in and try to alter his creation? In fact I understood it, but I wanted to instill some literary value into these science fiction myths. He had his own formula which worked. He was obviously saturated with science fiction, and he had a great following. So there I was getting on his nerves.

"In any case," he continues, "we developed these stories and somewhere along the line I began to get tired of having to go to him for approval of a story, because this wasn't my understanding of my function there. It's one of those things that no one wants to touch, because it could be a very serious problem. All you can do is ignore it and hope that the problem doesn't arise. Well, it did, and I began to commission stories without his approval."

Both creative talents weathered this rapidly intensifying storm for the next two months while plans were being laid to bring "In Thy Image" to the television screen, with much attention going to the scripts which would fill up the rest of the first thirteen put into work [once again, we refer you to the Appendix for full plot information].

Harold Livingston handed in his first draft teleplay of "In Thy Image" on October 20. Essentially the same plot as **Star Trek: The Motion Picture**, "In Thy Image" begins with Admiral James T. Kirk being asked to assume command of the Enterprise to stop a mysterious object that has wiped out three Klingon vessels and is on a direct heading for Earth. To this end, he reunites most of his original crew, and is assigned new members Xon, Decker and Ilia. Together, they head out towards deep space, learning en route of each other's strengths and weaknesses. A

"

I don't remember when I began to pierce the Roddenberry myth, but he and I suddenly started to have creative differences.

"

83

VOYAGER WILL CARRY "EARTH SOUNDS" RECORD

On the chance that someone is out there, NASA has approved the placement of a phonograph record on each of two planetary spacecraft being readied for launch next month to the outer reaches of the solar system.

The recording, called "Sounds of Earth," was placed Friday (July 29) aboard the first of two Voyager spacecraft scheduled to be launched to Jupiter, Saturn and beyond.

The 12-inch copper disc contains greetings from Earth people in 60 languages, samples of music from different cultures and eras, and natural sounds of surf, wind and thunder, and birds, whales and other animals.

The record also contains electronic information that an advanced technological civilization could convert into diagrams, pictures and printed words, including a message from President Carter.

teacher-pupil relationship quickly develops between Kirk and Decker, with the captain demonstrating strategic moments of command which only come from experience, and the younger officer forcing Kirk to open up his mind to new ways of thinking. Xon is fairly quickly accepted by the majority of crew members, with the exception of the man whose acceptance he most desires: Kirk. It's obvious that the captain is a bit prejudiced, expecting Spock to be at his usual station, and getting a bit testy when Xon doesn't respond exactly as his former comrade would have. This Vulcan, apparently, is going to have to *earn* Kirk's trust and friendship. Luckily he is well on his way by the time the mission ends.

The Enterprise eventually encounters Vejur, which turns out to be a Voyager space probe that left Earth hundreds of years earlier and achieved consciousness. It is now attempting to meet its creator, and doesn't believe that the "parasitical units" inhabiting the starship and Earth could possibly be the ones that created it. It's up to Kirk and his crew to convince it that mankind is a benefit to the universe, and not a plague to be exterminated.

Despite Spock's absence, "In Thy Image" works remarkably *better* than the first film did. Characters are given more depth than they had towards the original series' conclusion, and the addition of Xon, Decker and Ilia is truly beneficial. The only complaint is that Vejur is essentially talked out of destroying Earth, which seems somewhat anti-climactic when compared to the build-up we're given.

As Livingston was wrapping up his first draft, talk began that the character of Decker would somehow be done away with in the next draft, as the general consensus was: "Who needs two Captain Kirks?" What had started out as a solid addition to the crew, was turning out to be something of a headache.

"I think it would be very beneficial for us to determine as soon as possible whether or not the character of Will Decker will continue or be eliminated," said Livingston just before handing in his script. "Every story in work and those also in script contain Decker as a very integral character. If we're going to eliminate him, I think we had better move on it now to further save ourselves much unnecessary work re-writing, and writing around the elimination of that particular character."

The producer/writer handed in the script, and the reaction from Gene Roddenberry was immediate.

"I delivered it," Livingston recalls, "and Gene said, 'Good, you've done your job. Now just relax and I'll write the second draft.'"

In the meantime, Arthur Fellow, head of television production, issued a memo to Gene Roddenberry in which he discussed his and Michael Eisner's feelings regarding the first draft script.

"The return of **Star Trek** is an event in itself," wrote Fellows, "and we believe that this script really incorporates the elements that will be an extraordinary send off for the next 'five' years. The action and basic story are well conceived. However, at this rough draft stage a problem exists throughout in the arena of character and relationships."

Fellows believed that through the course of the script we never really felt the enormous weight that had been placed on Xon's shoulders, nor were we given the opportunity to see him win the respect of the crew. This situation, he felt, should be rectified in order for the public to accept this new and different Vulcan. In addition, the feud between McCoy and Xon (ergo, humanitarianism versus logic) should be dealt with more fully, filling the viewer with warm recollections of the McCoy-Spock relationship.

"In many ways we face a similar task with Decker," he wrote. " [If he's] going to be around for a long time, any intensifying of the emotions surrounding his existence and purpose on the ship will only aid in endearing him to all involved."

While feelings were strong regarding Ilia, it was generally believed that the character should not be bald. "Her baldness," pointed out the executive, "may really get in the way of the audience buying the intense relationship between Kirk and the woman. We would prefer to have Ilia with hair, keeping the bald girl but giving her some other function on the show." It seems that Gene Roddenberry had a somewhat similar struggle over twenty years ago, when network executives pleaded with him to get rid of "the guy with the ears."

"The storyline presented is quite special and extraordinary," Fellows enthused, "but somehow the ending seems to be too 'small' when we consider what led up to it. The slow, steady build-up of excitement and tension as this story unfolds is so effective that the ending deserves to soar. Right now, it is a bit anti-climactic. The final dialogue and moment when Ilia has convinced Vejur to save the servo-units is too convenient."

The main Voyager objective is to conduct a detailed scientific investigation of giant Jupitor and ringed Saturn, eleven of their moons and possibly Uranus, before leaving the solar system to journey nearly endlessly among the stars.

The messages on the record were designed to enable possible extraterrestrial civilizations who might intercept the spacecraft millions of years hence to put together some pictures of 20th Century Earth and its inhabitants.

"Because space is very empty, there is essentially no chance that Voyager will enter the planetary system of another star," said astronomer Carl Sagan of Cornell University. "The spacecraft will be encountered and the record played only if there are advanced spacefaring civilizations in interstellar space. But, as the beautiful messages from President Carter and Secretary-General Waldheim indicate, the launching of this bottle into the cosmic ocean says something very hopeful about life on this planet."

The idea for the record was formulated by Sagan and the repertoire was selected by an advisory committee of prominent scientists, musicians and

85

others. Sagan also was responsible for the plaques with a message previously sent into interstellar space aboard the Pioneer 10 and 11 spacecraft.

A phonograph record was chosen because it can carry much more information in the same space than, for example, the Pioneer plaques. In addition, 1977 is the 100th anniversary of the invention of the phonograph record by Thomas Alva Edison.

Each record is made of copper and is in an aluminum protective jacket. It contains, in scientific language, information on how the record is to be played, using the cartridge and needle provided. The record begins with 115 photographs and diagrams in analog form, depicting mathematics, chemistry, geology, and biology of the Earth, photographs of human beings of many countries, and some hint of the richness of our civilization. Included are schematics about the solar system, its dimensions and location in the Milky Way Galaxy, descriptions of DNA and human chromosomes, photographs of Earth, the Voyager launch vehicle, a large radio telescope and human beings in various settings and endeavors.

"Robert Goodwin's theory about the ending," muses Livingston, "is that I just pissed it away because I was so disgusted with the situation. I think the truth is that I couldn't come up with an ending. I just couldn't do it. The problem was that we had an antagonist so omnipotent that to defeat it, or even communicate with it, or have any kind of relationship with it, made the concept of the story false. How the hell do we deal with this? On what level? Everything pretty much worked in the story until we got to the ending. We tried all kinds of approaches, including aesthetic, theological and philosophical. We didn't know what to do with the ending."

Jon Povill, on the other hand, did. "We knew we had to have a big special effects ending," he says. "The problem of what was going to happen at the end and why it was going to happen, was one that plagued the script from the very start. The original treatment had a showdown between Vejur (although it wasn't called Vejur at the time) and Captain Kirk in which he draws a droopy daisy. Vejur recognizes that there is great power and value in this droopy daisy and flies off. Real deep. Then Gene came up with the idea of the machine dumping its data into Decker, with a light show of all the information it had accumulated. We were going to get all this amazing, incomprehensible stuff that Vejur had accumulated in its travels across the universe, and, of course, nobody could come up with these images. So that didn't work.

"It was pretty much my contribution," Povill goes on, "to say that the reason for what was happening was that this thing needed to go on to the next plane of existence; that it was transcending this dimension and going on to the next. It then became logical that the machine would need that human element to combine with. It was the only thing that could have made sense."

As Povill noted, Gene Roddenberry's rewrite of "In Thy Image" featured Vejur unloading its information into Decker, and then using the commander to transcend this dimension to enter another. Initial reaction to the script was not all that favorable from many of the people involved with the show.

"He did the script within a week," Harold Livingston explains. "Then he proudly brought it in, and there it was: 'In Thy Image, screenplay by Gene Roddenberry.' He gave it to us to read, and we read it. I was appalled and so was everyone else, Povill, myself, Goodwin and Bob Collins. He kept the structure that I created, but he did crazy things to it."

"Harold and I sat across from each other," Collins concurs, "and we asked each other which one of us was going to tell him that it wasn't quite right. Finally I said, 'Hell, I'm the director,' and walked out of the room."

It ultimately fell upon Harold Livingston to inform him of the situation. "I went in and said, 'Gene, this doesn't work.' Well, his face dropped to his ankles. Then I got wound up and told him *why* it didn't work. I said, 'When something works, you don't piss in it to make it better.' He was pretty stubborn about this and said, 'We'll give it to the front office.' About three days later, we had a meeting in Michael Eisner's gigantic white office. We sat at a round table, and at the meeting was Roddenberry, myself, Katzenberg, Eisner, Arthur Fellows and production people. Michael Eisner had two scripts, mine in a brown folder and Gene's in a yellow one. He balanced each in one hand and said, 'Listen, this is the problem. This (the yellow folder) is television, and this (the brown folder) is a movie, and frankly, this (brown) is a lot better.' Well, holy shit ... everybody was clearing their throats. There was the great man who had his feathers ruffled. After some heated discussion, it was decided to make Collins write a third draft using the best elements of both."

On October 31, 1977, Bob Goodwin noted that conversations between Bob Collins, Joe Jennings and Bill Koselka, the manager of Mission Support at Jet Propulsion Laboratories, had resulted in some new ideas about the ending of the script. Much of this was inspired by the transformation of Decker, as written in the Roddenberry screenplay, which had touched a chord with Collins.

"It began when Joe Jennings remarked that a key element in our story—the fact that Vejur has no knowledge of organic life—is incompatible with the facts," Goodwin related. "According to Joe, Voyager contains a great deal of information on mankind that was sent out specifically with that probe. After researching all the facts with Bill Koselka, I have managed to fit the true nature of the Voyager in with some elements for an ending I have been thinking of, and other elements that Bob Collins had mentioned."

In that conversation which took place on October 28, Goodwin queried Bill Koselka as to whether the signal from Voyager was being directed at an intelligent being.

"Right," replied Koselka. "Instructions how to play it back and get information off of the record. These are symbolic representa-

This is followed by spoken greetings in approximately 60 human languages, including a spoken message by Kurt Waldheim, Secretary General of the United Nations.

The Voyager record next includes a sound essay on the evolution of the planet Earth, including sounds of weather and surf, the Earth before life, life before Man and finally the development of human civilization.

The musical selections, which run to almost 90 minutes playing time, are representative of the cultural diversity of Earth, of many times and places, and include both Eastern and Western classical music and a variety of ethnic music. Included is music from Senegal, Australia, Peru, Bulgaria and Azerbaijan, as well as jazz and rock and roll. In the classical repertoire are compositions by Bach, Beethovan, Mozart and Stravinsky, as well as Javanese Gamelan, Indian Raga, Japanese Skakuhaci and Chinese Ch'in music. The entire 16 2/3-rpm record runs nearly two hours.

Because of the aluminum cover and the emptiness of interstellar space, the record is likely to survive more than a billion years. Thus it represents not only a message into space, but also a message into time, a point referred to in President Carter's message, which reads in part as follows:

"This is a present from a small distant world, a token of our sounds, our science, our images, our music, our thoughts and our feelings. We are attempting to survive our time so we may live into yours. We hope someday, having solved the problems we face, to join a community of galactic civilizations. This record represents our hope and our determination, and our good will in a vast and awesome universe."

Among the members of Dr. Sagan's Committee and others who played a major role in devising the Voyager record are Dr. Frank Drake, Cornell University; Dr. A.G.W. Cameron, Harvard University; Dr. Phillip Morrison, Massachusetts Institute of Technology; Dr. Bernard Oliver, Hewlett-Packard Corporation; Dr. Leslie Orgel, Salk Institute; Mr. Alan Lomax, Choreometrics Project, Columbia University; Dr. Robert Brown, Center for World Music, Berkley, California; Murry Sidlin, National Symphony Orchestra, Washington, D.C. and artist Jon Lomberg, Toronto, Canada. The record was produced by Timothy Ferris; the creative director was Ann Druyan, both of New York City.

tions that show how the signal is modulated or coded onto the phonograph record so that supposedly someone with intelligence could take that phonograph record, devise a scheme to get the information back and then learn something about the people on planet Earth."

He went on to explain that the recording contained greetings in over sixty languages and music from various time periods.

"Then there are sounds of waterfalls, wind blowing through mountains, ocean surfs," Koselka continued. "Things such as that on the phonograph record. And then there are two photographs like a TV recorder—like Universal put on their Laser Entertainment Center—that type of modulation. Those I don't know what they finally decided on, but there are a few scenes of typical things on Earth, and I don't know if people are included in it. I would guess so."

Goodwin then asked him if the memory banks of Voyager only contained technical information, to which Koselka replied that the only technical information would be gathered by the sensors.

"And information about how to program the spacecraft to save itself," he elaborated. "The reason it needs that type of information is because it takes so long to communicate with it because of the round trip light time—hours—so something could go wrong with the spacecraft, and by the time the information reached Earth it would instantly send the information back in a day or so. In the meantime, the batteries could short circuit something, burn it out or ruin the spacecraft. So the spacecraft has been programmed with intelligence to detect anything that's not right and put it into a safe condition, and then telecommunicate the information back to Earth while it has saved itself and while we decided what to do, and then we send up new instructions."

"With all the information within those redundant memory banks," Goodwin interjected, "is there nothing in there that relates to human, organic life?"

"That's true," he responded. "There's nothing that could tell anybody anything except about machines."

Robert Goodwin became intrigued. "How do our people get the information on that gold plate into those redundant memory banks?"

"What they could do somehow is use the computer on the spacecraft, assuming the machine is very intelligent up there, and program the banks to display that information, however they sense it."

Goodwin could see how all this would fit perfectly into the premise of "In Thy Image."

"For instance," Goodwin said, "we have already established that they have sent a number of probes aboard the Enterprise and one of them 'sees.' It could instruct the computer in the Voyager to have one of these seeing Probes focus on the gold plate."

"Right. By its eyes, depending on how much intelligence it has been given, read off the information ... read it back to the computer and the spacecraft."

"Yes," he concurred, "or at the same time we could program into these memory banks the code for decoding these grooves .... One other thought: at the moment when it releases all of this information to the computer about mankind, we're thinking of doing a short two-minute montage with flashes of things such as paintings and scenes and that sort of thing ... is that conceivable if that sort of thing is in the photographic record?"

"Yes," concluded Koselka. "I'll get a complete list of what's on it [see SIDEBAR], and you might use that type of thing."

When Bob Collins speaks of his ideas for the conclusion of "In Thy Image," he is justifiably proud.

"I thought it was a wonderful and spectacular idea for the end," he states candidly. "Decker sacrificed himself at the end of the picture, and unleashed a history of mankind. It would be a ten minute sequence where we would flash images of mankind since the dawn of the apes up till the present. These flashes of images would be all over the ship. All this would be accompanied by a musical montage of Beethovan and Bach. It was a grand idea and very ambitious, and I think it would have set off the end of it in a very spectacular manner. I remember that I wrote something to that effect, not particularly well I imagine, but that was my thought on how the picture should end.

"I was trying to deal with what this animal known as man really is, and essentially I was saying that man was pretty good," he adds. "It was the aesthetic approach, and no one argued with it."

Co-producer Bob Goodwin in particular was intrigued by the history of that particular scene.

"The plaque on Voyager should have been scarred," he recalls,

The record was prepared for NASA as a public service by Columbia records. Permission to use copyrighted material on the record has been given to NASA by the owners, also as a public service.

The first Voyager will be launched aboard a Titan Centaur rocket on August 20, and the second on September 1. They will arrive at Jupiter in 1979, Saturn and its rings In 1980, and possibly examine Uranus in 1986. The two spacecraft will be considered to have left the solar system when they cross the orbit of Pluto in 1989.

The Voyager spacecraft will escape the solar system at a speed of 17.2 km/sec (38,700 miles per hour), but this is a slow speed for interstellar distances. It will take at least 40,000 years before either spacecraft approaches another star—passing it at a distance of about one light-year (six trillion miles). Other predictable approaches to stars will occur in 147,000 and 525,000 years.

COPY OF

PRESIDENT'S MESSAGE

PLACED ON VOYAGER RECORD

This Voyager spacecraft was constructed by the United States of

America. We are a community of 240 million human beings among the more than 4 billion who inhabit the planet Earth. We human beings are still divided into nation states, but these states are rapidly becoming a single global civilization.

We cast this message into the cosmos. It is likely to survive a billion years into our future, when our civilization is profoundly altered and the surface of the Earth may be vastly changed.

Of the 200 billion stars in the Milky Way Galaxy, some—perhaps many—may have inhabited planets and spacefaring civilizations. If one such civilization intercepts Voyager and can understand these recorded contents, here is our message:

"This is a present from a small distant world, a token of our sounds, our science, our images, our music, our thoughts and our feelings. We are attempting to survive our time so we may live into yours. We hope someday, having solved the problems we face, to join a community of galactic civilizations. This record represents our

slowly at first, "by one small meteorite which obliterated the 'OYA' and a small portion of the coded markings below. In other words, a large portion of the coded markings have remained intact. When Kirk comments on the engraved markings, Ilia tells him that 'It is not known' what the meaning of the markings is ... 'The true meaning is known only by the Creator.' Kirk reacts to this."

Goodwin pauses again, almost as though he's gathering his energy, and then dives into an analysis of this concluding sequence from the script.

"There are some serious problems here," he begins. "If the Vejur is 'satisfied that the servo-units do not accept the Creator', then why bother to send Kirk and Xon back to the Enterprise? Why not just wipe them out right there? ...and the crew of the Enterprise ... then go on to Earth and blast them all? This could have been a good place to give William Shatner one of those scenes—as Bob Collins had pointed out—he does so well. A solid, dramatic argument between Kirk and the Ilia android could be very exciting. The computerized logic of the machine against the passion and wiles of the human. Kirk would do anything to get back to the Enterprise and to Earth. He would counter logic with logic. He would confuse Ilia with appeals for sympathy. In the end, he would lie. He has to get to Archives and prove what he's saying about Vejur.

"The idea is that Kirk would remember that the Voyager plaque includes a vast amount of visual and audio records of human existence. What better proof to Vejur of mankind's role in its creation than evidence which is itself a part of Voyager? Kirk must get to Archives Building to obtain the information that will enable the Enterprise to unravel the code of the Voyager plaque, and, at the same time, be a means of feeding that data directly into the computer of the Voyager."

According to Goodwin, Kirk would naturally make his way to the Archives, while Decker is attempting to physically transmit the information with his tricorder. Xon would finally transmit to the Voyager computer an order to project a "seeing" probe which would appear and begin to focus on the plaque, closing in on the microscopic etchings.

"Then you have Decker under assault," he continues with enthusiasm. "We see the myriad of images of information with which Voyager is bombarded. Here we would have done Bob Collins' montage of music and sights of mankind. Since it is the information recorded on Voyager in 1977, we wouldn't have had to have worried about carrying the message into the 23rd Century or beyond. We could have even included portions of the message from President Carter and U.N. Secretary General Waldheim. This would have given us an exciting, inspiring moment—a crescendo of audio and visual impressions."

Bob Collins himself adds even more to the imagery. "We see Decker making his way toward Voyager," he says, "but as he does, he is consumed by the energy of Vejur caught in an energy field more powerful than a million volts of electricity, and becomes himself an energy field. He becomes fused to the ship, melted into it. His consciousness, his mind, his memories, become part of Vejur. In a pyrotechnic display of light and sound, the history of mankind is propelled, projected, onto the walls of the ship. A whirling cascade of pictures—the pyramids, the Parthenon, the Mona Lisa, Versailles, Jesus, Mohammed, Ghandi, the Grand Canyon, the Alps—the wonders of the Earth bombard the inside of the ship as Jim Kirk beams himself aboard. We see Kirk surrounded by the sights, the visuals whirling around him, over him, into him. The sights, the sounds: Beethovan, Schubert, Bach, the music of the world. The sights of all history—huge, giant events all playing upon Kirk as Vejur assimilates and understands. It has become Decker. Decker has become it, and the neutron bombs [threatening Earth] are withdrawn. Kirk is allowed to return to the Enterprise with Ilia. The ship, and Decker, leave Earth to seek the universe as Decker's voice, a thousand times amplified as part of Vejur, tells Kirk, 'There's beauty here ... the universe before us. Eternity.'"

Certainly an incredible and profound image, and one probably unparalleled in cinematic history.

Production designer Joseph Jennings concurs with this, stating that, "The idea was a bit more in the **Star Trek** image, which is a good deal more specific than what wound up in the feature picture. That thing was just so abstract. You know, there's always the trouble in science fiction that the creative people in the field turn to those responsible for its realization and say, 'We want something people have never seen before.' Frequently you find yourself in the trap that if you can imagine it, their reaction is 'That's not far enough out. How did you know about it?' It's sort of a strange line of thinking. Maybe they think they'll push you one step further. What it frequently results in is stasis, and you

hope and our determination, and our good will in a vast and awesome universe."

Jimmy Carter
President of the United States
of America
The White House
June 16, 1977

VOYAGER MESSAGE

OF UN SECRETARY GENERAL

"As the Secretary General of the United Nations, an organization of 147 member states who reperesent almost all of the human inhabitants of the planet Earth, I send greetings on behalf of the people of our planet. We step out of our solar system into the universe seeking only peace and friendship, to teach if we are called upon, to be taught if we are fortunate. We know full well that our planet and all its inhabitants are but a small part of the immense universe that surrounds us and it is with humility and hope that we take this step."

Kurt Waldheim

reach a point where you just can't go any further. If that's not acceptable, then of course they have to go somewhere else. It almost feels to you, the person responsible for it, that anything you can imagine is not acceptable, simply because you can imagine it. It's a Catch 22 kind of situation, and I think that's why you lost that ending."

LANGUAGES HEARD

ON VOYAGER RECORD

Sumerian, Spanish, Turkish, Swedish, Akkadian, Indonesian, Welsh, Ukrainian, Hittite, Kechua, Italian, Persian, Hebrew, Dutch, Nguni, Serbian, Aramaic, German, Sotho, Luganada, English, Bengali, Wu, Amoy (Min dialect), Portugese, Urdu, Korean, Marathi, Russian, Vietnamese, Polish, Telugu, Thai, Sinhalese, Netali, Oriya, Arabic, Greek, Mandarin, Hungarian, Roumanian, Latin, Gujorati, Czech, French, Japanese, Ila (Zambia), Rajasthani, Burmese, Punjabi and Nyanja

SOUNDS OF EARTH ON VOYAGER

Whales, Planets (Music), Volcanos, Mud Pots, Rain, Surf, Crickets, Frogs, Birds, Hyena, Elephant, Chimpanzee, Wild Dog, Footsteps and Heartbeats, Laughter, Fire, Tools, Dogs, domestic; Herding sheep, Blacksmith shop, Sawing, Tractor, Riveter, Morse Code, Ships, Horse and Cart, Horse and Carriage, Train Whistle, Tractor, Truck, Auto Gears, Jet, Lift-off Saturn 5 Rocket, Kiss, Baby, Life signs—EEG, EKG and Pulsar

By the time early November 1977 came along, production of "In Thy Image" was scheduled to begin in just a matter of weeks. It seemed that nothing was going to interfere with **Star Trek**'s return. On November 10th, Roddenberry shot a memo off to Bob Collins, detailing William Shatner's comments regarding the "*second* draft script" (a statement, if one chose to read into it, which already was indicating the competitive creative struggle that would be waged between Roddenberry and Livingston throughout production).

"Bill suggests that Kirk might participate with Xon in the first realization that the Vejur machine is alive," wrote Roddenberry. "Sees no dramatic objection in Xon coming up with the first realization, but does believe that Kirk should immediately see what Xon is talking about and help flesh out the theory ... He comments that the major sag in the story comes between the Enterprise being grabbed by Vejur and the final resolution of the story. He suggests that this is the area in which pages should come out ... These comments, to me, seem to be sound and certainly worth serious consideration."

On November 15th, Harold Livingston, working as professionally as he felt he could, despite the fall-out with Roddenberry, submitted yet another writer's status report, pointing out that a variety of final scripts would be coming through over the course of the next few weeks.

"As of this date, two first draft scripts have been delivered and six are expected momentarily. Of the four projects awaiting script assignment and/or further discussion," he said, "two we feel need considerable work to make them viable. Our status at this point, therefore, is nine hours committed to script, leaving us with two hours open. We will select those two either from the remaining four one-hour projects, or we will exercise our remaining two hours to put into work an entirely new project from an in-house story. We are closed to submissions at this time.

"Of those episodes now in work, I am particularly looking forward to 'Practice in Waking,' by Richard Bach, which really promises to be a landmark **Star Trek** film. 'Tomorrow and the Stars' by Larry Alexander is another for which I have great expectations. This is the one that takes Kirk back to the time of Pearl Harbor, involves him in a fascinating—and unrequited—

> "
>
> As of this date, two first draft scripts have been delivered and six are expected momentarily.
>
> "

93

love affair. Summing it up, then, we are—as of this date at least—in fair shape."

By the end of the month, Bob Collins had submitted his rewrite of the Livingston and Roddenberry drafts of "In Thy Image," and this one did not go over very well at all.

"His was a total disaster," says Livingston.

On December 1, Jon Povill expressed his own opinions to Gene Roddenberry. "I feel that the characters and dialogue are wrong throughout much of the script," he admitted. "Specifically: Decker is petulant and totally unsympathetic for the first two-thirds of the script. Then, with no transition, and, more importantly, with nothing happening directly to or with him that would cause him to undergo this transformation, he abruptly mellows into a team player.

"McCoy has no meat. There are no revealing glimpses of the true depth and character of the relationship between Kirk and McCoy. Instead, McCoy wanders in and out, dropping sarcastic comments at inappropriate moments.

"Also, the character of Vejur needs fleshing out. Vejur is our antagonist and *must* be developed as fully and consistently as if it were a humanoid. The script attempts to represent Vejur as an incredibly intelligent and complex living being. If we wish to avoid comparisons to Nomad (from the episode 'The Changeling'), we must see evidence of this intelligence and complexity that go beyond its mastery of technology. Despite its unfamiliarity with our variety of life forms, it must come to anticipate some of our moves at least as readily as a computer might anticipate the moves of a human opponent in a chess game.

"Our relationship with Vejur is a game of lion and mouse in which the resourcefulness of the mouse has intrigued the lion sufficiently to keep it around for a while. The lethal paw is only a whim away. Fortunately for us, machine life forms are not prone to whims. In all fairness to Bob, I would have to say that none of the drafts to date have succeeded in truly bringing Vejur to life. If you can develop him as fully as you did Tasha [actually the nickname for an android duplicate of Ilia created by Vejur], I think we will have a blockbuster script.

"In my opinion, in order to make Vejur consistent, there are two conflicting areas of his personality which need to be reconciled in order to understand his motivations and avoid an aftertaste of

> **The character of Vejur needs fleshing out. Vejur is our antagonist and *must* be developed as fully and consistently as if it were a humanoid. The script attempts to represent Vejur as an incredibly intelligent and complex living being.**

contrivance. These areas are curiosity and prejudice. These could be reconciled by virtue of the wedding of Voyager to the original machine race. If the original machine race had stagnated because of the rigidity of its value system, then the original meeting with Voyager would have some of the characteristics of an unfulfilled Mormon striking up a friendship with a hedonist. This exploratory pilgrimage that Vejur is making would then be something that it is not entirely comfortable with.

"Perhaps Vejur's prejudice might be more believable if it did have dim memories of having been at one time in control of humanoid beings. Beings who had manipulated and controlled them. Beings from whom they sought independence in order to develop as they wished. Eventually they fought and defeated their own masters, only to stagnate without the spark of humanoid inventiveness. The machines, left to their own devices, could *do* anything, but they had never learned a why for any of it.

"We have been saying the Voyager's programming gave the machine race purpose. Perhaps it would be better if we thought of it as new purpose, the old purpose having been to be free of humanoid control. Thus, when Vejur gets into space, the new purpose (to learn) comes into conflict with the old purpose whenever they come across carbon-based life. Vejur might believe (with considerable justification) that metallic-base machine life evolved from carbon-base machine life in much the same way we believe that we evolved from apes. As far as Vejur is concerned, carbon-base life, however complex, is at least a step or two down the evolutionary ladder from machine (metallic) life. Vejur's lack of respect for carbon-base life forms could stem from having been initially designed and built by a race that displayed a similar lack of respect for 'lower' life forms. This attitude programmed into the early machines eventually justified the machines takeover once they had developed to the point where they were more capable than the humanoids who had built them. Thus, the lack of respect was perpetuated as prejudice through the centuries. The new viewpoint that Vejur must get by virtue of its union with Decker is a tremendous respect for all lifeforms. Of course in order to accomplish this, Decker must be portrayed in a manner befitting a man who has respect for all life forms.

"Maybe I'm crazy, but I don't think the above would entail very much more exposition than we've already got. As it stands now, Vejur's justification for the eradication of humanity is vague at best. Whether this particular back story works for you or not, I

> " The lack of respect was perpetuated as prejudice through the centuries. The new viewpoint that Vejur must get by virtue of its union with Decker is a tremendous respect for all lifeforms. "

think it definitely necessary to insert *some kind* of additional background information that will enable our audience to understand Vejur so that it is not just another 'incredible monster from space' adversary."

What's fairly amazing about the above comments, as well as many of the others which have been discussed in considerable detail throughout this text, is that they all serve as proof that the creative minds behind "In Thy Image"/**Star Trek: The Motion Picture** recognized the script's shortcomings. They were able to point out alternatives which could have made the final film considerably better.

Yet when the film eventually reached theaters, we could see that little had been done. Why? The most common answer is Roddenberry's determination to get *his* vision of the story on the screen.

Gene Roddenberry's values lay in his knowledge and experience. Now if he had imparted that and allowed the professionals to do their job, they might have had a picture. Rewriting was compulsive with him; he simply could not live with himself knowing that someone else was writing **Star Trek**," states Harold Livingston matter-of-factly. "In December of '77, Roddenberry and I were really at each other's throats. My contract was up around that time and I quit before they could fire me. I knew there were too many problems. The film was in preproduction, and they had gone back to basically what I wrote, with Collins as a writer, restoring much of what he had left out, but little of Gene's."

Interestingly, Livingston would ultimately quit the **Star Trek** project three times, and would eventually have to fight with Roddenberry over the screenplay credit on the film. He was always coaxed back by the Paramount brass. For the moment, however, he believed that he was leaving the realm of the 23rd Century behind him forever.

As the new year came in, so did the decision—though not an absolute one—to turn the **Star Trek II** television series into a feature film. Jon Povill, who had taken over the writers status reports after Livingston's departure, pointed out that "all the scripts that we have in hand are in very good shape, and should Paramount at some point decide to proceed with the series, I feel that we have here the nucleus of an excellent first season."

On January 19th, Jeff Katzenberg stated that "We are currently analyzing all of the aspects necessary to move forward with **Star Trek II** as a theatrical motion picture. Unfortunately, much information—premature and potentially destructive to our long-range planning—already has leaked out to the media and the public. This has become most alarming, even though we are appreciative of such widespread interest in the project and aware of its future value to us [a classic case of understatement, considering that **Star Trek** has become a billion dollar industry for Paramount].

"It therefore becomes imperative that *no* information regarding the film be given out at this time. I must emphasize how essential it is that information concerning this show not now be given out by those associated with it in any capacity. The project at its present stage can suffer seriously. And the success of a properly

> **"**
>
> Rewriting was compulsive with him; he simply could not live with himself knowing that someone else was writing **Star Trek.** In December of '77, Roddenberry and I were really at each other's throats. My contract was up around that time and I quit before they could fire me.
>
> **"**

97

timed, well-coordinated future public relations campaign can be jeopardized."

The decision to produce **Star Trek: The Motion Picture** came about for a number of reasons.

The three networks, fearful of any new competition, reportedly lowered their advertising rates. This made it less viable for Paramount to begin their fourth network.

At the same time, Paramount's initial fear that **Star Wars** had been an one-time phenomenon had been nullified by Steven Spielberg's success with **Close Encounters of the Third Kind**. They now believed that science fiction could appeal to movie audiences of the 1970's and '80's.

"Obviously the real reason the **Star Trek** film finally got the go-ahead was because of **Star Wars** and **Close Encounters**," says Alan Dean Foster, whose "In Thy Image" was destined to serve as the basis for **Star Trek: The Motion Picture**. "After that, and this is supposition on my part, everybody started running around like crazy. I think that after being told, 'Yes, we're doing a series, no we're doing a movie, yes we're doing a series, no we're doing a movie,' suddenly somebody said *'YES,* we're doing a movie,' and everybody hears money. Everybody ran around trying to find something so that they could get started *right away* with budgeting and casting. Unfortunately, once it became a big budget movie, I didn't get so much as a phone call. Not an invitation to come down to the set, or a request for suggestions."

As was the case with Harold Livingston, the attempt was made to have his name removed from the screenplay, including his story credit. This, also as with Livingston, changed when Roddenberry was threatened that the matter would be referred to the Writer's Guild.

"I'm the kind of guy who believes that a handshake bonds a deal," Foster says, "and I had seen the shooting script some time later and my name wasn't even on it. I had called my agent, who has been around since the nickelodeon days, and said, trying to keep my blood pressure down, 'What's going on?' And he said, 'Oh, that's nothing.' 'What do you mean nothing?' 'That's just the way they do things. Nobody's mad at you or anything, it's just the business.' 'Well, it's not my business.' My agent eventually suggested I file for solo story credit, because I did 98% of the writing of the treatment, and I did. Then Harold Livingston called me and said, 'Just because Roddenberry is being a son of a

Obviously the real reason the **Star Trek** film finally got the go-ahead was because of **Star Wars** and **Close Encounters.**

bitch, doesn't mean you should be one too.' I thought about it and said, 'You're right,' so I called the Guild and told them that I was interested in having it read 'Story by Alan Dean Foster and Gene Roddenberry.' Because, as I freely admit, it was based on his one page story idea. I then get this very strange letter back from the Guild saying that Gene Roddenberry is off some place recuperating. He's very tired and busy, and he really doesn't have time for this. I just laughed. Is this real life or is this kindergarten?"

Ultimately he did receive sole story credit, but the experience was so discouraging that he and his wife left California for Arizona.

Apparently they put you in the shark cage. And either you learn how to fight with the other sharks, or you go back into the goldfish bowl, and I guess I belonged in the goldfish bowl.

So, after thousands and thousands of man-hours of work, why was the television series concept of **Star Trek II** finally abandoned in favor of a feature film? The answer to this seems much simpler then they labyrinth that led to this point.

"It was a combination of things," explains Gene Roddenberry. "Five years ago, Paramount began looking at the remarkable rerun of the **Star Trek** series—and they began to say, 'Well, gee, maybe we *do* have something here.' And it resulted in, four years ago, my checking into the studio with the idea of putting together a **Star Trek** feature. At the time, the plan was just to do a modest-budget feature; and they were convinced they had a sufficient audience. But we couldn't come up with a script that Paramount really liked. Paramount wasn't that much into science fiction at the time. I think a lot of studios at the time had a rather simplistic view of science fiction—rocket ships and blasters and high adventure—the kinds of things that, really, you saw in **Star Wars**, though probably with a few more half-nude women. I just wasn't interested in doing a space pirate type of show—a film is just too great an exertion of time and energy. The concepts I was working in and trying to get by at the same time had some fairly complex and, I thought, daring thematic material. And that just kind of shook them up, because they weren't thinking of science fiction as being a really heavy thematic thing. We finally ended up starting to do it as a spectacular for television to open up a new series. But about that time, **Star Wars** did come along and showed that there was, indeed, not only the audience that they thought might be there, but a rather unusual-sized one at that ... They have been moving toward it for a number of years. Not fast enough to suit me, nor with a large-enough budget, but they were moving."

"When 'In Thy Image' became a feature," adds director Bob Collins, "we were given a budget of about eight million dollars. Somewhere around that time we were talking about special effects. Roddenberry and I went down to the Pacific Theatre and sat down for what I think was a noon performance of **Close Encounters**. We came out and were both pretty blown away by the film. I turned to him and said, 'Well, there goes our low budget special effects.' After **Star Wars** and **Close Encounters** you couldn't do those kind of special effects anymore. That meant a whole new thinking and a whole reorganization of the production and concepts. They needed a great deal more money and time, and there were only a few people who could do it.

> **"**
>
> Roddenberry and I went down to the Pacific Theatre and sat down for what I think was a noon performance of **Close Encounters**. We came out and were both pretty blown away by the film. I turned to him and said, 'Well, there goes our low budget special effects.'
>
> **"**

"We spoke to John Dykstra and Robert Abel, and they chose Abel," he recalls. "So he came on board and decided that he would make it into a Robert Abel production. His budget, which had originally been one or two million dollars, suddenly jumped to seven and ten million dollars. The budget kept rising, and Paramount was getting more and more nervous as it kept pumping more and more money into it."

As the budget on the film rose, Collins began to suspect that his time with the project was limited. What he did not expect was a political back-stabbing.

"We were preparing to make this picture," he says, "but the writing was on the wall. I was a television director who had not done a feature film at that time. It was evident that they were going to hire somebody who was used to working with big budget special effects. Paramount wasn't brave about such things, so I called up Jeff Katzenberg and said, 'You're going to replace me, right?' He said, 'No, Bob, never. Take my word for it, Bob. Trust me.'

> His budget, which had original-
> ly been one or two million dol-
> lars, suddenly jumped to seven
> and ten million dollars. The
> budget kept rising, and Para-
> mount was getting more and
> more nervous.

"Then my agent," Collins adds, "who at that time handled Robert Wise, called up and said, 'Look, we've got an offer for Robert Wise to replace you on the picture.' Apparently Paramount couldn't remember that we both had the same agent, so I called up Jeff again and said, 'Look, are you going to replace me?' He said, 'Absolutely not. Never. You're absolutely staying with the project.' I pointed out that Robert Wise and I had the same agent, so he said, 'If Robert Wise doesn't do it, then you are absolutely going to do it. ' I kind of laughed about that for a while. I knew it would happen sooner or later. They wanted to get somebody in place before they fired me. So they got Wise, and the first step was to redecorate my office.

"I was more angry about the way it happened. I could understand them wanting someone else when the budget escalated to twenty million dollars, but I wish they would have been nicer about it and said, 'Look, these are the facts of the situation.' But Paramount's not the only place in town that works that way. I was angry at Katzenberg. Anyway, and this isn't sour grapes, I never really thought the film did all that it could do. It wasn't as good as it could have been. This is not against Robert Wise, because given the circumstances, I don't know how anybody could have done. But I didn't think the script was very good in any case."

He's quick to add that any anger he felt was not really directed at Gene Roddenberry.

"Gene would often say about the script, 'This isn't **Star Trek**,'" Collins reflects. "One could argue that it may not be **Star Trek**, but it's good. At the same time, you had to realize that on a human level, on a personal level, that he was wrapped up in it. His whole way of defining himself was involved with the series and with this project. I don't think any of us ever felt very angry at him. We all wanted to help him realize his ambition, and we wanted to make a good picture too. Paramount was kind of holding a gun to his head, saying that they were going to do it, and then they weren't going to do it. That tension, I think, flowed through all of us. I'm not sorry about calling somebody an a— hole if that's what I think they are, but I liked Roddenberry and I always felt sympathetic towards him and the project."

So Bob Collins left the film, with actor David Gautreaux, who was to have played the young Vulcan Xon, soon to follow. At that time, casting had been going on for someone to portray Decker, but this was put on hold for a time.

"They went with Robert Wise as director," offers Bob Goodwin as an explanation for why he never cast the role. "Gene and I were never really informed of what the steps of the deal were. It turns out that Robert Wise is used to getting producing and directing credit. Apparently he would not accept a producer, so Gene Roddenberry was moved to executive producer and I was asked by Gene and the studio if I would stay on as associate producer. I didn't want to spend a minute of my life doing that. I was an associate producer ten years earlier, and it was taking a step backwards, especially facing two years of production. So I left.

"What really upset me about all this," and Goodwin really seems to be punctuating each word at this point, "is that at the same time I had a pilot that had gotten a go-ahead. I had developed it under the Playboy job. It was a wonderful script, but I was having severe problems with the director, who was shooting down in New Orleans. I was the executive producer and had hired a producer, but no one was watching the store down there. The dailies were coming in and they were just terrible. So I wanted to go down there and try to pull it together, because I saw the handwriting on the wall. But the guys at the feature department threatened that if I went down to New Orleans, they would take me off the picture. At the same time, they were negotiating a deal that would have me off the picture anyway. So what ended up happening was that by the time I finally got word on the Robert Wise deal, I immediately got on a plane and went to New Orleans, but

The guys at the feature department threatened that if I went down to New Orleans, they would take me off the picture. At the same time, they were negotiating a deal that would have me off the picture anyway.

by that time it was just too late. Not only did I end up not doing the **Star Trek** film, but I ended up with a terrible pilot that did not sell. So there I was, literally out on the street. I came to work one day and they had taken my name off the door. My stuff was packed in boxes in the hall and the janitor told me I had to be off the lot in twenty minutes.

"That's the way they handled it," Goodwin concludes. "That's the kind of thing that can destroy you. I began to wonder, 'What did I do wrong?' Luckily, someone I knew with money had been waiting for me to leave Paramount, because he wanted to start a company with me. Thank God for small miracles."

In March of 1978, one of the largest entertainment press con-
ferences of all time was held, its purpose to announce that production would soon be commencing on **Star Trek: The Motion
Picture**. Directing would be the highly-esteemed Robert Wise,
with the entire original cast, including Leonard Nimoy, reprising
their television roles.

The fictional character of Lieutenant Xon was gone, as were the
very real Robert Goodwin, Bob Collins, Harold Livingston (at
least temporarily) and numerous others who had devoted nearly a
year of their lives to a project which would never see fruition.
Right or wrong, the revival of **Star Trek** was the only thing that
really mattered to those who remained involved with the project.

"We're trying to develop the movie's inherent theme more,"
Roddenberry told those gathered, emphasizing his vision of the
future. "We want to evoke the feeling that Kubrick tried to get
across in **2,001**. We want to make audiences leave the theatre
thinking, 'Who are we? What are we? Where are we going as human beings in this universe?' "

Powerful questions. Unfortunately, the resulting answers were
not as satisfying.

The myth had been slightly tarnished, and by the time the film
made it to the screen, a great portion of the audience would wonder what all the fuss and bother had been about in the first place.

105

THE SCRIPTS

"IN THY IMAGE"

Teleplay by Harold Livingston

Story by Alan Dean Foster

Kirk reunites most of his old crew to save Earth from the threat of Vejur, the returning Voyager space probe that has achieved consciousness and is hell-bent on destroying the carbon-based units which infest the planet of its creator. Essentially Vejur is attempting to capture God. This plot, of course, has been discussed in detail throughout this volume.

"STAR TREK II"

Treatment by Jon Povill

A mass of pulsating crystal plasma contains the mangled, apparently lifeless bodies of Kirk and the Enterprise crew. Then, the bodies heal, slowly disappear and rematerialize on the Enterprise. Kirk and company learn that the Enterprise had been studying a black hole when suddenly there was a surge of energy. Some crew members are missing.

After they find Starfleet missing, Chekov announces that they've all been dead for eleven years. As they change course for Earth, the Enterprise encounters a Rigelian starship, whose captain does not recognize the Enterprise and informs Kirk that Earth has never been a part of the Federation of Planets.

They head straight for Earth while on Vulcan, Spock utters Kirk's name and remembers parts of a former life. At that exact moment, Kirk orders the Enterprise's course to be altered for Vulcan.

While the ship is in orbit, Kirk beams down, and is greeted warmly by Spock. The two transport to the Enterprise, breaking orbit as a pair of Vulcan cruisers approach. They realize the universe has been altered.

When they arrive on Earth, there is no sign of Starfleet Command. The city is nothing as it had been; people are uniformly dressed, the city itself a conglomeration of structures, lacking the beauty of the 23rd Century they had known. Meanwhile, Uhura locates the survivors of the shuttle mission, who, like the crew of the Enterprise, were spared from the time-changes.

Kirk and Spock beam down to their wilderness habitat, and are informed that shortly after the scientists arrived, the planet's surface was suddenly covered with a vast, ugly urban sprawl, and the world was abruptly populated by a "race of mindless automatons who do nothing but eat, sleep and perform their designated functions within the social order." They ask about Scotty, and are told that he had been working in a special laboratory in Munich, studying the time gap. Scotty, they realize, is somehow the source of the time-shift.

The Enterprise travels backwards in time. Kirk, Spock and one of the scientists (Yeoman Roberts) beam down to a Munich that "looks notably different than what they expected." They discover a replica monument of the laboratory they seek, commemorating the initial appearance of the "Mediator" in 1937. They are 27 years too late! According to the people they question, the Mediator brought peace and optimism to the world, cured diseases and fed the hungry. He can be found at the League of Nations headquarters in Geneva.

They beam over to Geneva, and learn that the Mediator is a computer.

Scott is responsible for the future time alteration.

Because of Scott's interference, the world is slave to a computer.

When Kirk, Spock and McCoy find Scotty, he explains that his first experiments had proven successful and, five years later, he attempted time travel to prevent the black hole incident, but something went wrong and he suddenly found himself surrounded by German soldiers and found himself in a position to change history. He developed potent medicines and agricultural systems, saving lives and eliminating famine.

Kirk tells him about the future and Scotty explains that he could use his knowledge to alter even that time period. Spock disagrees, stating that they need the dilithium crystal which serves as an ornament on the man's dining table so that they can go to 1937 and correct history. Scott will not go, stating that this is his world now. He gives Kirk the crystal, reasoning that even if the captain straightens everything out, perhaps this alternate reality will exist on another dimensional plane.

They beam back aboard and begin their journey. Unfortunately, Enterprise's engines will only take them back as far as 1940. Phasers lash out and destroy specified targets in both Geneva and Munich. A moment later, the Enterprise itself explodes.

A younger and happier Kirk, Spock and Scott appear at Starfleet Command in the proper time frame of the 23rd Century. Spock informs the Command Officer that his time gap calculations were mistaken, and investigation of the black hole will not be necessary.

The Enterprise crew has been rewarded by the plasma entity—actually the evolved form of humanity in the alternate future—with another chance at life.

"THE CHILD"

Written by Jon Povill and Jaron Summers

The Enterprise passes through a mysterious cloud, and as it does so, a strange form of energy penetrates the starship's hull and proceeds to Lieutenant Ilia's quarters. A glow envelops her entire body and she begins to moan with pleasure. When she awakens the next morning, she informs Doctor McCoy that she is pregnant.

Within three days, Ilia gives birth to a beautiful girl, who begins to age rapidly. In a matter of hours she is ten years old, and growing older. While McCoy tries to discover what's happening, the Enterprise is afflicted with one near-disaster after another, every one of which is averted at the last moment by the child (named Irska, which, in Deltan, means "bright light"). Then, Kirk learns that the molecular structure of the Enterprise's hull is breaking down and will turn to dust in a matter of hours.

Xon performs a Vulcan mind-meld on Irska, and learns that she must be transported directly into a bright light which has been following the ship. This is done, and the hull's breakdown is instantly reversed.

Pondering the situation, Kirk, Ilia, McCoy and Xon conclude that, in some strange way, the Deltan had served as Irska's first womb, while the Enterprise served as the second. The aliens had arranged it so that the child would learn all about human emotions, wants, needs and the ability to make sacrifices for loved ones, before it metamorphosized into a higher life form.

"The Child" is one of the best **Star Trek II** scripts, with a fascinating story and characters who react quite touchingly. Note the difference in subject matter from the original series. Odds are that in the sixties it would have been impossible to do a story involving immaculate conception.

This particular script holds a special place in Jon Povill's heart.

"One of the keys to me becoming story editor on **Star Trek II** was that 'The Child' had to be written in a week," Povill recalls with a laugh. "I had Jaron Summers do a first draft, and then I had to do a pretty complete rewrite. It had to get into shape for shooting, and the way that script came out would determine whether or not I could be the story editor."

He got the job.

"THE SAVAGE SYNDROME"

Written by Margaret Armen and Alf Harris

Decker, McCoy and Ilia investigate a derelict vessel in orbit around a lifeless planet. On board, they find that the crew had killed each other in savage ways. But why?

Meanwhile, a space mine detonates near the Enterprise, unleashing an energy which attacks the neural impulses of the crew, and transforms them into savages. Primitive forces drive their every move. The trio return to the Enterprise to try to reverse the mine's effects before the starship and her crew are destroyed.

"The Savage Syndrome," like the original series' "The Naked Time," was important because it was a shipboard story (thus keeping the budget down) that took the characters in new directions, while also providing plenty of action. One interesting character bit involves the savage Kirk, who, paralleling his more "controlled" counterpart, automatically takes a position of command amongst the primitives.

"Gene Roddenberry was very close to the show," says Margaret Armen. "Alf and I went in with three stories, and in the end it was 'The Savage Syndrome' that he liked, because he was looking for **Star Trek** stories that were really different."

"PRACTICE IN WAKING"

Written by Richard Bach

The Enterprise comes upon a sleeper ship with only a single passenger. Scotty, Decker and Sulu beam over to investigate and discover a woman in suspended animation. Scotty accidentally touches a control panel and the three collapse to the deck, only to reawaken in ancient Scotland without memory of their lives aboard the starship. In the past, they meet with the same woman and protect her from the mobs who claim that she is a witch.

Meanwhile, on the Enterprise, McCoy discovers that Scotty, Sulu and Decker's life signs are growing progressively weaker. His prognosis is that the longer they remain in this dreaming-state, the closer they come to actually dying. Kirk and crew must somehow awaken them before they drift off into final sleep.

"Getting Richard Bach to work on **Star Trek** is a real score for the show," Harold Livingston said at the time. "His story should make one hell of an episode."

Livingston's assessment was typical. Despite never making it to script form, "Practice in Waking" was one of the most popular story ideas among the **Star Trek II** crew. They felt that Richard Bach would add a certain amount of class to the series and pave the way for new directions.

111

"TO ATTAIN THE ALL"

Written by Norman Spinrad

While trapped in another dimension, the Enterprise is boarded by a blue-skinned alien who refers to himself as The Prince. He tells Kirk and the others that if they prove worthy, mankind will be the recipient of the ultimate gift: the attaining of the "All."

Kirk reluctantly accepts the demand that Decker and Xon, representative of their respective species, be the ones who'll attempt to unlock the Prince's secret. If Kirk refused, the starship would never be allowed to return home. The duo appear in a maze-like structure with a planetqid, and are told that their goal awaits them at the other end. They proceed, and at mid-journey take note of a bizarre switch in personality traits: Xon utilizes human intuition while Decker applies Vulcan-like logic to problems. They ultimately reach the other end of the maze and the glowing sphere that awaits them. Xon reaches out to touch it, and his mind is assaulted by an energy unlike any encountered before. Then, with the Vulcan serving as a conduit, the alien intelligence within the sphere begins spreading its influence through the Enterprise. It rapidly possesses the majority of the ship's crew and engineers a permanent switch of personality traits. It becomes rapidly apparent that they're all becoming part of *one* mind.

The intelligence inside the sphere plans to force the humans to merge with the All. The All, after acquiring physical bodies, could go deep into space and merge with all intelligent beings in the galaxy. The Prince believes this is fair, for even though humanity will lose its individuality, it will gain immortality. The price, naturally, is too high. It's up to Kirk (and eventually Decker) to save all.

While the intellectual subtext of "To Attain the All" is commendable, there are certain similarities to the original series' "Return to Tomorrow." That episode featured Sargon and his followers, who were eager to utilize human bodies to travel through the universe. It's a bit disconcerting to see the repetition of ideas, but Spinrad, an award-winning SF author, would undoubtedly have done a highly creative job of developing this treatment into a teleplay.

"THE PRISONER"

Written by James Menzies

The bridge crew is understandably shocked when the image of Albert Einstein appears on the main viewscreen, requesting that the starship help him. Einstein explains that he and many other Earth scientists were kidnapped and kept alive by a "storage battery" on an alien planet. While Kirk doesn't believe that he is *truly* speaking to Einstein, the captain's curiosity is aroused. He orders the ship to that world.

While in orbit, six scientists from Earth's past (circa the early 20th Century) appear in the transporter room. Xon is quick to discern that they aren't living beings, but rather highly realistic illusions. Now aware of the trap they've been caught in, Kirk orders the Enterprise to break orbit. The ship cannot. Beaming down to the planet, the captain comes face-to-face with Logos, the alien behind the charade. His goal is to assume the identity of all human life, beginning with Kirk and his crew. This, Logos feels, is only fair considering that humanity is such a savage race, constantly living under the threat of nuclear annihilation. Kirk counters that the Earth Logos speaks of is ancient history. The alien refutes this, insisting that man will never change.

A battle of wills between the Enterprise crew and Logos follows, with the destiny of humanity hanging in the balance.

The storyline seems very much like those of several episodes from the original series.

"TOMORROW AND THE STARS"

Written by Larry Alexander

Due to a transporter malfunction, Kirk is sent back in time to Pearl Harbor in 1941—mere days before the Japanese attack. At first, he materializes in a ghost-like state, unable to touch or be touched by anything.

Kirk meets Elsa Kelly, a woman unhappy with her marriage to career-Army husband Richard. Initially frightened by Kirk's appearance, she tries to accept his story on face value. Meanwhile, Xon and Scotty attempt to "yank" Kirk back to the Enterprise. That fails to bring him back but makes him solid again. This, in turn, leads to Kirk and Elsa falling deeply in love. The dilemma arises of whether or not Kirk should alter history by warning her of the imminent Pearl Harbor attack, or merely depart with Decker and Xon when they locate him.

Despite strong similarities to "City on the Edge of Forever," and the question of how a transporter malfunction could propel someone back through time, "Tomorrow and the Stars" would have been an effective **Star Trek II** episode. Perhaps most important is that it's written with a more current sensibility with characters and dialogue updated from the old show.

An interesting moment occurs shortly after the transporter malfunction, when the ghost-like Kirk screams out, "Xon, what have you done to me?" The line seems to indicate Kirk's bitterness that Xon isn't Spock.

"Oh yeah," laughs writer Larry Alexander, "but that's only because I was able to take it one step further. In other words, Xon

113

is not Spock, even though I considered him Spock from a character point-of-view. So, there is a little resentment there. It seemed the 'logical' thing to do."

This script began when Gene Roddenberry gave Alexander "The Apartment," a story he had written for the aborted **Genesis II** series. Alexander came up with "Ghost Story," in which Kirk and the landing team beam down to a planet that lies in ruins. There, they discover highly advanced technology, but no sign of a living civilization. Kirk enters a science lab and is projected backwards in time, where he encounters a pair of scientists. These people have developed a device to scan the mind. On a human, however, it operates quite differently.

Hooked up to Kirk's brain, the machine causes him great agony. Suddenly the demon from within his mind, the Id, materializes and destroys all life on the planet (thus resulting in the destruction that the crew finds in the future).

Alexander freely acknowledges the debt that "Ghost Story" owes to **Forbidden Planet**, but points out that it goes beyond that film.

"I thought it was a wonderful story idea to have Captain Kirk responsible for the *death* of a planet," he enthuses, "and it's the one step beyond **Forbidden Planet** that had never been dealt with. It makes it much more human and, to me, much more of an interesting irony. That's the kind of material I think is interesting, and I was shocked when Gene Roddenberry said he *didn't* want to go with it."

It has been suggested that saddling Kirk with a planet's death wasn't the right thing to do to such a heroic series character.

"In effect, it wasn't *his* doing," Alexander differs. "He asked them not to do it. I was *very* strict about that. He didn't volunteer to do this, and when he realized what was going on, he did everything possible to stop it. All of that, I think, holds up on that basis. I was thinking very strictly about what happened to Kirk in many episodes where things didn't turn out the way he hoped. That's what makes **Star Trek** so wonderful.

"As heroic as Kirk was," he notes, "through no fault of his own, hard choices had to be made. In Harlan Ellison's story, Kirk has to allow Edith Keeler to die. It's a gulp at the end of the show, and it's like that when the people of this planet find that it's *his* demons which have destroyed their world, not theirs. It makes it that much more ironic."

Roddenberry preferred instead that Kirk go back to Earth's past and chose Pearl Harbor as the time and place.

"It seemed a very obvious choice," muses Alexander. "Pearl Harbor is good, though, because you could use footage from various war films, which would work. But I didn't want to have the responsibility, because the story works as a story. It's like sending somebody back in time to kill Adolph Hitler in the crib, and he does it. The only irony you can have is his coming back and them saying, 'Why didn't you kill Kowalski like we asked you to?' History would be the same, but somebody else would do the job.

"You want to go back in history?" he concludes rhetorically. "Give me an event and I'll do it. The story is the same no matter what."

"DEVIL'S DUE"

Written by William Lansford

Responding to a distress signal from a solar system "that shouldn't exist," the Enterprise arrives at Neuterra. Kirk, Xon, McCoy, Sulu, Ilia and Chekov beam down to the surface. They find a paradise, and a profound sadness amongst its people.

Meeting with the world's most blessed member, Zxoler, Kirk comments on the planet's beauty. The elderly man announces that all life on Neutrerra will be destroyed in 20 days, which is the reason for the distress signal. One thousand years earlier (when Zxoler was a young man), the people had reached a point where their science outstripped their wisdom to control it. As a result, the planet was ecologically raped and their civilization lie on the verge of extinction. Then, a being identifying itself as Komether appeared in answer to their prayers. It promised them 10 centuries of prosperity in exchange for their planet at the end of that time.

Unfortunately the prosperity of the planet extinguished the civilization's desire to develop. They never came up with a way to leave their world, choosing, instead, to enjoy paradise. Now their time is almost up.

While Kirk feels sympathy for their plight, he points out that the Enterprise is not equipped to transport more than a handful of extra passengers; *any* additional aid would arrive too late. Kirk finds himself, as a representative of the Federation, defending the planet in a trial against Komether, who just might be the Devil himself. The captain suspects this demon may have been created from the Neuterrans' mind.

In Jon Povill's opinion, "Devil's Due" could "work very well. It had all the elements necessary for a very exciting, involving episode."

"This was essentially 'The Devil and Daniel Webster,'" said Harold Livingston. "The story has been developed to a point where we all feel it will be a most exciting **Star Trek**."

115

"DEADLOCK"

Written by David Ambrose

Commodore Hunter informs Kirk that the Enterprise will partake in war game activities. The captain is to take orders from Starfleet Science Adviser Lang Caradon. Knowing the man's reputation, McCoy points out that the tests will likely be an experiment in behavior control. This does not please Kirk.

Continuing games of manipulation ensue, culminating in a very real near battle-to-the-death between the starship and Starbase 7. Kirk, Decker, McCoy and Xon beam over to the base to see what they can do to prevent the imminent destruction. They ultimately discover that key Starfleet personnel, including Hunter and Caradon, have been replaced by alien beings. They reveal that the Federation is near their territory, which concerns them deeply. It's their intention to create hostilities among humans so that they'll eventually destroy themselves and never infect the aliens' part of the galaxy.

It's up to Kirk and company to defeat the scheme, while convincing the aliens that the Federation poses no threat.

"David Ambrose is a British writer whom we had at one time considered for the two-hour premiere," explained Livingston. "His story, 'Deadlock,' concerns the Enterprise and a starbase involved in war games which turn out to be much more serious and which truly test the mettle of all our characters, our procedures and the bravery of our Enterprise crew. This should also be an extremely exciting story."

"Deadlock" begins as a highly imaginative suspense thriller, with no one really knowing truth from fiction. The idea of training exercises "gone wrong" is an intriguing one, but unfortunately echoes the familiar refrain: an alien intelligence offended by humanity's barbarity tries to destroy mankind.

The concept of "gods" striking against man—an old standby used by Gene Roddenberry—may have been added to the story at the request of others. Ambrose's earlier treatment, "All Done With Mirrors," offered the same story with a *different* resolution. In this scenario, Caradon belongs to an underground organization which plans to overthrow the Federation. The struggle between a flagship and a starbase was just one of many accidents triggered by "dedicated fanatics" in key Starfleet positions, all pledged to sacrifice their lives for the cause.

"THE DARKER SIDE"

Written by Jerome Bixby

The Enterprise arrives at the planet Demonos, a world deserted a millennia earlier. A landing party beams down to find pentagrams and other occult symbols carved into the planet's ruins. Additionally, they learn of animal-like humanoids residing in the hill territories, the descendants of this world's former natives.

Upon completing their investigation, the landing party beams up and unknowingly brings along a disease that spreads rapidly throughout the crew. The disease brings forth the dark side of each crew member infected.

As the disease spreads, a very large landing team decides to start a separate society, but is quickly captured by the natives. Kirk and Scotty rescue them via shuttlecraft, but the captain becomes afflicted. He counteracts the disease by sheer force of will. Going down to the planet's surface, Kirk combats the Devil himself, described as being huge, horned and evil. The alien thrives on and breeds negative emotions within human beings. Kirk, through "some particle of scientific truth contained in occult belief," defeats him and escapes with the Enterprise.

"LORDS OF LIMBO"

Written by Jerome Bixby

The Enterprise delivers supplies to the planet Limbo, a prison world complete with its own set of laws, industries, social structure and government. Beaming down, Kirk and the landing party fall captive to the society due to an inmate who hopes to cause enough commotion to prompt a Federation investigation.

Further complications arise. Penal staff members allied with the Klingons have been stealing vital medical supplies as a recreational drug.

Bixby wrote that the story would be light melodrama, with "much opportunity for fast action plus humorous touches in the colorful subcultures through which Kirk moves."

"SKAL"

Written by Jerome Bixby

A Klingon named Skal, the equivalent of an Einstein among his own people, wishes to defect to the Federation in order to help create peace between his people and them. Kirk, naturally, accepts him with open (albeit cautious) arms.

Skal utilized a simulation chamber to equip him for life on Earth, and it is there that McCoy discovers that Skal is quite unknowingly carrying a germ which would have come to life once he reached Earth, but now thrives due to the simulated atmosphere. The Klingons believed Skal would defect, and made the proper preparations. The virus quickly multiplies and begins claiming the lives of crew members. Nothing effects it. Skal, realizing that one life for 400 is fair exchange, asks that he be transported into space. Kirk reluctantly agrees to this sacrifice, but changes his mind at the last moment. Tying the computer into the transporter, they continuously beam Skal into a trailing shuttle and back again until the organism phases out of his system.

Action, according to the author, would come from a pair of Klingon cruisers who at first claim they want Skal back, then attack when they realize Kirk is destroying their micro-organism.

"ONLY A MOTHER"

Written by Jerome Bixby

Billed as a comedy, this story deals with the ship being equipped with an energy-to-matter converter. The device was installed on a matriarchal planet and the ship's computer has been affected.

The Enterprise itself actually "reproduces," creating a dozen miniature versions of itself which trail the "mothership." When the Klingons utilize a tractor beam to grab one of the smaller vessels, Kirk finds himself in the position of having to steal it back before they can study it to learn the secrets of the Enterprise.

"SMALL WAR"

Written by Jerome Bixby

While confronting a Klingon vessel within the Neutral Zone, Kirk is stunned to find himself alone on the bridge, with giant aliens peering in through the main viewscreen. Attempting to utilize the turbolift, the captain finds himself on the Klingon bridge. The commander of that ship, Kos, also finds himself baffled by the events. The pair declare a truce to work together. A turbolift deposits them in an elegant room.

The duo find their way out of the room and abruptly appear on a desert planet. The giant aliens disappear, but Kirk and Kos run for their lives when an "alien bloodhound" pursues them. Eluding it, they help each other through various other threats before returning to the same elegant room. The giant aliens finally explain that by cooperating intelligently, Kirk and Kos proved their civilized status. Free to leave, they suddenly find themselves on their respective ships. No battle begins between them.

"MARLA"

Written by Jerome Bixby

While the Enterprise delivers supplies to Marcus X, Marla, the daughter of the colony's leader, falls for Kirk. Soon, the ship finds itself locked into orbit, as one disaster follows another.

Marla makes approaches to Kirk, but he politely backs away. He wants to be friends and nothing more.

He is stunned when his wishes begin to come true. Eventually he finds himself home in Iowa. Everything appears *exactly* as he remembers it, right down to his old puppy.

Kirk snaps himself out of this fantasy and tells Marla that despite the magic tricks, things can't work between them. She departs in tears. Kirk quickly falls victim to a poltergeist attack. As he investigates further, Kirk discovers Marla's power source, a crystalline computer built by aliens to "gratify their every need."

Kirk defeats Marla. Turning the powers in a positive direction, the colonists plan to use the crystal to provide rain for crops, construct new buildings and help in education.

"PANDORA'S PLANET"

Written by Jerome Bixby

Responding to a distress signal in an unexplored part of the galaxy, the Enterprise arrives at a planet inhabited by the survivors of a Federation vessel that crashed 30 years earlier. They're under attack from highly advanced reptilian creatures intent on driving humans from the world.

This story ultimately showcases a classic case of sociological contamination. The crew of the downed vessel broke the Prime Directive and taught the reptilian savages about the Federation and that organization's technical abilities.

One thing should be pointed out about Jerome Bixby's various **Star Trek II** story ideas: they were designed to serve as *premises*, not final stories. Merely launching points, they could have been developed into full-fledged stories.

"LORD BOBBY'S OBSESSION"

Written by Shimon Wincelberg

Starfleet sensors detect a possible penetration of the Neutral Zone by a Romulan vessel. The Enterprise is ordered to investigate. At the Zone, they encounter a smaller ship and a humanoid who identifies himself as Lord Bobby, actually Lord Robert Standish, the third Early of Lancashire, kidnapped from Earth by aliens at the beginning of the 20th Century. Somehow, these vanished aliens made him immortal. Bobby is thrilled to be among humans again.

As soon as the visitor boards the starship, five Romulan vessels surround and fire upon the Enterprise. They disable the warp drive. Kirk must convince the Romulans that the Enterprise isn't on a hostile mission, while at the same time dealing with the potential threat of Lord Bobby. An examination by Dr. McCoy, reveals Bobby as an alien whose real purpose is unknown.

"Lord Bobby's Obsession" may have made an interesting episode, placing Kirk and his crew in the midst of two potentially explosive threats and utilizing the sadly under-employed Romulans.

"ARE UNHEARD MELODIES SWEET?"

Written by Worley Thorne

A landing party arrives on the surface of a planet within the Haydes star cluster. It searches for the remains of the U.S.S. St. Louis, which reportedly crashed there. Xon locates the ship's log, and, via tricorder, learns that the crew had been afflicted by a strange delirium from the planet and had piloted the ship into the atmosphere.

Decker mysteriously disappears, while the Enterprise crew seems to contract the disease. Kirk must return to the ship, while also locating Decker. The commander is held prisoner by an alien race with illusionary abilities, who force him to live out one sexual fantasy after another. Their lives exist only *within* illusions, resulting in their world falling to ruins. They face extinction, and that' s where the Enterprise personnel come in. The aliens plan to "manufacture" hormones to enhance their dream worlds, and prolong their race. The Earthlings serve as suppliers.

Kirk and his crew eventually learn that this race had once been extremely savage, but by focusing on the unreal, they suppressed their true nature. Fantasy sex fills a void in their lives, but they no longer produce the necessary hormones. As a result, their old aggressions are returning.

Kirk must resist temptation and rescue Decker, while McCoy (again) searches for a cure to the rapidly spreading disease.

"Working on **Star Trek** was something I very much wanted to do," says writer Worley Thorne, who would ultimately pen the "Justice" episode of **The Next Generation**. "I began my career the year that the original show started, and I felt as though I missed out because I wasn't established enough to write for it. This was an opportunity to do something I had always wanted to do."

"KITUMBA"

Written by John Meredyth Lucas

The Enterprise embarks on a potential suicide mission to the Klingon homeworld to prevent an intergalactic war. Aided by a warrior named Ksia, who doesn't believe either side could survive such a conflict, they pass safely to the planet's surface. There they encounter the leader of the Klingon people, the Kitumba, a child destined for greatness.

Kirk does his best to convince the Kitumba that an invasion of Federation space would be disastrous for both sides. The captain seems to be winning over the youth, but realizes that there's no clear-cut way to end the potential war. The Enterprise crew, falls into the midst of a power struggle between the ruler and his most trusted aides. That struggle will determine whether the ultimate war begins.

"Kitumba" is filled with enough thrills, plot twists and adventure to keep the reader guessing. Of all the scripts written for **Star Trek II**, it is this final entry that would *still* make an exciting feature film, delving into an area previously unexplored.

The Klingons had been used in a variety of episodes and feature films, but never to as great effect as they are here. To his credit, John Meredyth Lucas has taken previously established facts and expanded upon them to such a degree that as to create a very real Klingon society, far removed from their previous image as one-dimensional heavies.

Producer Harold Livingston had said at the time, "I think 'Kitumba' is very exciting, visually interesting and dramatic. It should be one hell of a show. [My notes] on it are really very minor, which illustrates the excellent flow of the story. So go with it and good luck."

Lucas himself is justifiably proud of this particular effort.

"I wanted something that we had *never* seen before on the series," he says, "and that's a penetration deep into enemy space. I then started to think of how the Klingons lived. Obviously for the Romulans we had Romans, and we've had different cultures modeled on those of ancient Earth, but I tried to think of what the Klingon society would be like. The Japanese came to mind, so, basically, that's what it was, with the Sacred Emperor, the Warlord and so on."

The World's Only
Official

COUCH
POTATO
BOOK
CATALOG™

Please note:
You must be a certified couch potato* to partake of
this offering!

* To become a certified couch potato you must watch a minimum of 25 hours a
day at least 8 days per week.

From Happy Hal...

Star Trek
Gunsmoke
The Man from U.N.C.L.E.

They all evoke golden memories of lost days of decades past. What were you doing when you first saw them?

Were you sitting with your parents and brothers and sisters gathered around a small set in your living room?

Were you in your own apartment just setting out on the wonders of supporting yourself, with all of the many associated fears?

Or were you off at some golden summer camp with all of the associated memories, of course forgetting the plague of mosquitoes and the long, arduous hikes?

The memories of the television show are mixed with the memories of the time in a magical blend that always brings a smile to your face. Hopefully we can help bring some of the smiles to life, lighting up your eyes and heart with our work...

Look inside at the **UNCLE Technical Manual**, the **Star Trek Encyclopedia, The Compleat Lost in Space** or the many, many other books about your favorite television shows!

Let me know what you think of our books.

And what you want to see.

It's the only way we can share our love of the wonders of the magic box....

Selection

> HAL SCHUSTER

Administration

> JACK SCHUSTER,
> COUCH POTATO

Customer Service

> PHYLLIS SCHUSTER

From The Couch Potato...

I am here working hard on your orders.

Let me tell you about a few new things we have added to help speed up your order. First we are computerizing the way we process your order so that we can more easily look it up if we need to and maintain our customer list. The program will also help us process our shipping information by including weight, location and ordering information which will be essential if you have a question or complaint (Heavens Forbid).

We are now using UPS more than the post office. This helps in many ways including tracing a package if it is lost and in more speedily getting your package to you because they are quicker. . They are also more careful with shipments and they arrive in better condition. UPS costs a little more than post office, This is unfortunate but we feel you will find that it is worth it.

Also please note our new discount program. Discounts range from 5% to 20% off.

So things are looking up in 1988 for Coach Potato.

I really appreciate your orders and time but I really must get back to the tube...

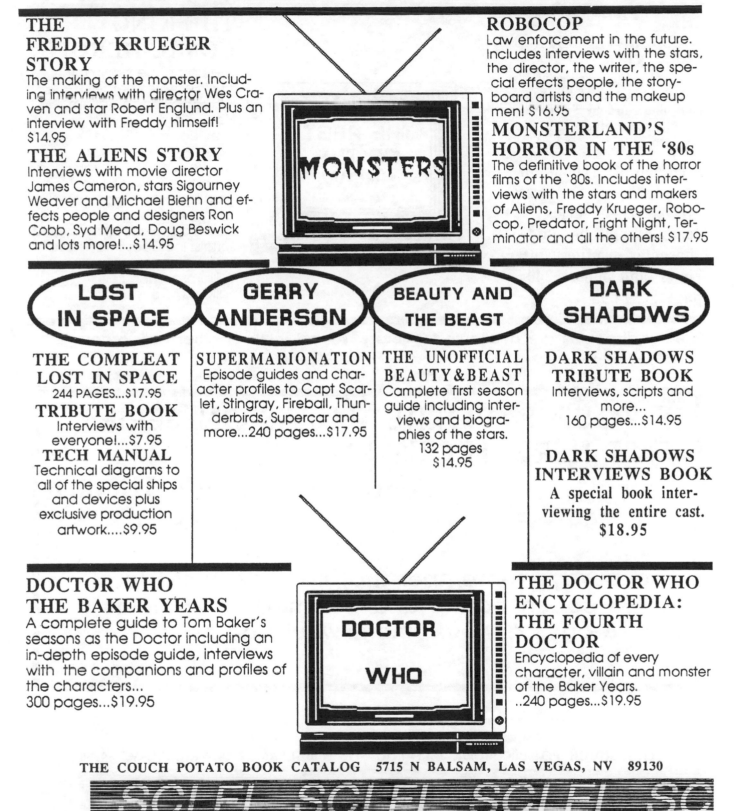

THE COUCH POTATO BOOK CATALOG 5715 N BALSAM, LAS VEGAS, NV 89130

THE ILLUSTRATED STEPHEN KING

A complee guide to the novels and short stories of Stephen King illustrated by Steve Bissette and others...$12.95

GUNSMOKE YEARS

The definitive book of America's most successful television series. 22 years of episode guide, character profiles, interviews and more...240 pages, $14.95

THE REST OF THE SHOW

THE KING COMIC HEROES

The complete story of the King Features heroes including Prince Valiant, Flash Gordon, Mandrake, The Phantom, Secret Agent, Rip Kirby, Buz Sawyer, Johnny Hazard and Jungle Jim. These fabulous heroes not only appeared in comic strips and comic books but also in movies and serials, Includes interviews with Hal Foster, Al Williamson and Lee Falk...$14.95

Special discounts are available for library, school, club or other bulk orders. Please inquire.

IF YOUR FAVORITE TELEVISION SERIES ISN'T HERE, LET US KNOW...
AND THEN STAY TUNED!

And always remember that if every world leader was a couch potato and watched TV 25 hours a day, 8 days a week, there would be no war...

THE COUCH POTATO BOOK CATALOG 5715 N BALSAM, LAS VEGAS, NV 89130

Boring, but Necessary Ordering Information!

Payment: All orders must be prepaid by check or money order. Do not send cash. All payments must be made in US funds only.

Shipping: We offer several methods of shipment for our product.

Postage is as follows:

For books priced under $10.00— for the first book add $2.50. For each additional book under $10.00 add $1.00. (This is per individual book priced under $10.00, not the order total.)

For books priced over $10.00— for the first book add $3.25. For each additional book over $10.00 add $2.00. (This is per individual book priced over $10.00, not the order total.)

These orders are filled as quickly as possible. Sometimes a book can be delayed if we are temporarily out of stock. You should note on your order whether you prefer us to ship the book as soon as available or send you a merchandise credit good for other TV goodies or send you your money back immediately. Shipments normally take 2 or 3 weeks, but allow up to12 weeks for delivery.

Special UPS 2 Day Blue Label RUSH SERVICE: Special service is available for desperate Couch Potatos. These books are shipped within 24 hours of when we receive your order and should take 2 days to get from us to you.

For the first **RUSH SERVICE** book under $10.00 add $4.00. For each additional l book under $10.00 and $1.25. (This is per individual book priced under $10.00, not the order total.)

For the first **RUSH SERVICE** book over $10.00 add $6.00. For each additional book over $10.00 add $3.50 per book. (This is per individual book priced over $10.00, not the order total.)

Canadian and Foreign shipping rates are the same except that Blue Label RUSH SERVICE is not available. All Canadian and Foreign orders are shipped as books or printed matter.

DISCOUNTS! DISCOUNTS! Because your orders are what keep us in business we offer a discount to people that buy a lot of our books as our way of saying thanks. On orders over $25.00 we give a 5% discount. On orders over $50.00 we give a 10% discount. On orders over $100.00 we give a 15% discount. On orders over $150.00 we give a 20% discount. Please list alternates when possible. Please state if you wish a refund or for us to backorder an item if it is not in stock.

100% satisfaction guaranteed. We value your support. You will receive a full refund as long as the copy of the book you are not happy with is received back by us in reasonable condition. No questions asked, except we would like to know how we failed you. Refunds and credits are given as soon as we receive back the item you do not want.

Please have mercy on Phyllis and carefully fill out this form in the neatest way you can. Remember, she has to read a lot of them every day and she wants to get it right and keep you happy! You may use a duplicate of this order blank as long as it is clear. **Please don't forget to include payment! And remember, we** *love* **repeat friends...**

■■■■■■■■■■■■■■■■■■■■■■■■■■■ **ORDER FORM** ■■■■■■■■■■■■■■■■■■■■■■■■■■■

_____ The Phantom $16.95
_____ The Green Hornet $16.95
_____ The Shadow $16.95
_____ Flash Gordon Part One $16.95 _____ Part Two $16.95
_____ Blackhawk $16.95
_____ Batman $16.95
_____ The UNCLE Technical Manual One $9.95 _____ Two $9.95
_____ The Green Hornet Television Book $14.95
_____ Number Six The Prisoner Book $14.95
_____ The Wild Wild West $17.95
_____ Trek Year One $10.95
_____ Trek Year Two $12.95
_____ Trek Year Three $12.95
_____ The Animated Trek $14.95
_____ The Movies $12.95
_____ Next Generation $19.95
_____ The Lost Years $14.95
_____ The Trek Encyclopedia $19.95
_____ Interviews Aboard The Enterprise $18.95
_____ The Ultimate Trek $75.00
_____ Trek Handbook $12.95 _____ Trek Universe $17.95
_____ The Crew Book $17.95
_____ The Making of the Next Generation $14.95
_____ The Freddy Krueger Story $14.95
_____ The Aliens Story $14.95
_____ Robocop $16.95
_____ Monsterland's Horror in the '80s $17.95
_____ The Compleat Lost in Space $17.95
_____ Lost in Space Tribute Book $9.95
_____ Lost in Space Tech Manual $9.95
_____ Supermarionation $17.95
_____ The Unofficial Beauty and the Beast $14.95
_____ Dark Shadows Tribute Book $14.95
_____ Dark Shadows Interview Book $18.95
_____ Doctor Who Baker Years $19.95
_____ The Doctor Who Encyclopedia:The 4th Doctor $19.95
_____ Illustrated Stephen King $12.95
_____ Gunsmoke Years $14.95

NAME:_____

STREET:_____

CITY:_____

STATE:_____

ZIP:_____

TOTAL:_____ SHIPPING_____

SEND TO: COUCH POTATO, INC.
5715 N BALSAM, LAS VEGAS, NV 89130